Wake Up, Darling

A Novella

Kristina Stangl

ISBN: 978-1-963232-00-4

First Edition
Cover Art: Romance Novel Covers Now
Library of Congress Registration Number: TXu002439662
Printed in the United States of America

WAKE UP, DARLING

DEDICATION

To my family and my readers.

And to everyone looking for a second chance, it's never too late to find your true happily ever after.

WAKE UP, DARLING

CONTENTS

Also by Kristina Stangl

The Enchanted Forest Saga:

The Curse of the Dark Horseman

The Sleeping Knight

The Emerald Prince

Silverheart:

Cupid's Serenade

Sex, Lies & Politics:

The Ambassador's Wife

Wake Up, Darling

My Life is a Soap Opera

Kill Me, Kiss Me

www.kristinastangl.com

CHAPTER 1

Once Upon a Coma…

With the sun flashing across my face, I struggle to adjust my eyes. But in truth, I can't *open* them, even if I wanted to. But it's not limited to just my eyes. It's also me moving my hands, too. And my legs. And my feet. And my toes. And my arms. And my fingers. It's *everything*. It's my entire body all at once, because I'm *paralyzed*.

Sadly, it took me a long time to come to this conclusion. But lo and behold, I am, indeed, paralyzed. In fact, I'm currently in a deep coma and everyone around me assumes the worst. That I'm lying on death's door. That in a matter of days… *no*… *hours*… and I'll most likely be declared as dead. Except I'm not. I'm *not* dead. I'm still here!

Strangely enough, I can hear them, but they *can't* hear me. I listen to their loud chatters and gentle whispers. I hear the doctors and the nurses coming in and out, all checking on me periodically. And they've been gossiping about me, too.

Whether I want to or not, I do hear their worries. How tragic my life must have been, according to them. That, for a young woman of thirty years of age, to be in the current vegetative state that I'm in. To be married to a wealthy senator and yet, for all the money in the world, I still lie unconscious in this bed. Even as a world-famous romance author, I, myself, could never have written such a tragic tale. And yet…

There was an accident. An accident that I can't seem to remember, no matter how much I struggle to recall. Something happened to me and whatever it was, it brought me here. To this very hospital. And now, as I lie in this bed, alone with only my silent thoughts and the sounds of my environment, I'm left wondering one question: why didn't I die?

For some reason, God spared my life. Even with all of the morphine pumping into my body to help me heal, I still can't recall what brought me here… and that alone makes me feel so upset.

No, upset isn't the right word. Instead, I'm *angry*. Better yet, I'm *furious*. I'm furious, because while the world perceives me to be in a coma, I'm still wide awake. Or at least, awake on the inside. Awake and silently listening to my surroundings. Hearing both the good and the bad, all around me.

My main visitors have primarily been the nurses. Mainly females. They cry for me. Many of them were my fans, who previously read all of my romance novels. I can hear their cries, and their well wishes. I know that they all mean well. And truly, I am grateful that my novels have brought them much joy and comfort. That, should I die right here, today; then at least my novels will continue to live on. Some piece of my legacy to pass on into the future. A future absent of any children of my own. *An unfinished life.*

Although I'm aware that I'm indeed, married; but in truth, I can hardly remember my husband. He's like a blackened blur. Both him and his face. But regardless, I do know that he *exists*. I can hear the nurses speak of him, time to time. From what I've gathered, he's a senator. Wealthy, young and handsome.

But has he come to visit me, as of lately? I'm not entirely sure.

However, there's been one man, who's the exception. In fact, he visits me quite often. I can hear him, always weeping. Grieving. His cries of despair might be soft and silent, but I do feel his tear droplets whenever they land upon my face. In truth, it's one of the few exceptions that I can actually *feel* against my entire body. *His endless tears.*

Whenever he enters into my room, the nurses all leave. Often times, he pulls a chair by my bedside and holds my hand. Surprisingly, I can *feel* his touch. It feels warm, nice and safe. But the only problem is that I *can't* move my hand to embrace his, in return. Oh, how I wish that I could! Not being able to touch him, truly feels like hell on earth! It's so unfair and cruel! Oh, how fate cursed me so!

Apart from holding my hand, he doesn't speak much. Honestly, he really doesn't need to. It's not like I can carry a conversation with him, anyways. But either way, he sits there. Silently. Peacefully. Sometimes for only a few short minutes and other times, for several hours on end.

Is he, my husband? I'm not entirely sure. He must be, right? Who else would bother to sit by my constant side, if not for him?

But whomever he is, he does bring me great comfort. Whether he's death or my husband, I don't care. But I do crave his touch. His attention. His affection. I relish on his surprise visits, whenever he comes. And when he's gone, I'm saddened by his absence. Even though I can't speak or touch him, I still *miss* him.

Sometimes, when I'm alone, I often wonder about him. Specifically, of what he looks like. I must have known him in my past. I must have. But then again, my memories are very limited.

Apart from my childhood, career and marital status, everything else is a darkened blur. And if it wasn't for the nurses' gossiping around me, then I'd have never have known that I'm married or that my husband is a senator. Sadly, I suppose this accident of mine really did destroy my memories after all…

Again, when my stranger is gone, I genuinely miss him. Even into the late hours of the night, I continue to fantasize about his appearance. Tall or short? Muscular or chubby? Blonde or brunette? Blue eyes or brown? A doctor or a scholar? A businessman or another senator? My husband or someone… *else?*

Mystery, after mystery, after mystery. Whomever my stranger is, I am forever grateful to him. I'm grateful, because apart from the hospital's medical staff, he's the only other person who continues to visit me on a regular basis. He's the only one holding my hand. The only person who encourages me. Motivates me. *Cries for me.*

Again, he doesn't speak much. But there's one phrase that he always utters. Over and over… and over again…

Wake up…

Wake up…

Wake up…

Wake up… *darling…*

His words are spoken like a prayer. He wishes for me to awaken from this coma and to be fair, I do, too. If only to catch a glimpse of his face.

But the truth is, I am awake. *Wide awake.* It's just that my body isn't. My eyes refuse to open, even though I want it to… oh, so desperately! But even when I command it to do so, it still doesn't obey. One way or another, my own body refuses to listen to me... it's like a violent war raging inside of me... and I'm struggling to win this battle...

But apart from my own internal struggles, his voice remains buried in my mind, as my constant motivation. The way he says the word *darling*, it's so touching. It's uttered, using a sweet and tender melody. Like that special word is just for *me*. A private word shared only between him and myself. That my name might be Karly Summers, but to him, I'm his one and only...

DDDDaaarrrlllliiinnnggg...

He stretches the vowels and elongates the consonants of this special word, all from the tip of his tongue. He wants me to awaken. So desperately. I can feel it by the sounds of his deep voice. He's trying to enchant me. To encourage me. Anything to have me wake up from this God forsaken coma!

And his words do encourage me. I try. Each day, I try to open my eyes. I practice using every ounce and fiber of my muscles. And one day, I know that I'm going to win this battle. I am going to wake up from this death sentence. I am going to recover. I will overcome my own weakened body, by the sheer power of my mind. I am determined to succeed. I am not a failure, but a fighter. And one day soon, I will open my eyes and rise again!

Because I've decided that this stranger is not death, but my savior. An angel who is desperately trying to keep me here on this earth. To stay alive. To recover. To reunite back with him. To simply *be with him*.

And so, for the next few days, I concentrate. I stay focused. I might still be too weak to wiggle my toes or my fingers, but I know... *I just know…* that I can, at the very least, open my eyes. And if I can open my eyes… then I can finally see him…

And then, on one sunny Sunday, I do. At long last, I finally do open my eyes and once I do, I see a man with bright blonde hair staring back at me and smiling…

CHAPTER 2

You're My Husband?

"Good morning, honey," says the man with a golden crown for his thick head of hair.

This strange blonde man is seated right next to me, and he's holding my hand. Whomever he is, I don't recognize him at all.

"The doctor and the nurses tell me that you've opened your eyes already once before," he says. And then, he takes in a deep breath and tells me, "Karly, you've suffered from a major injury. And as a result, you might be suffering from limited memory loss. Now, you might not recognize me, just yet. But please don't be alarmed or scared. Dr. Khan believes that if you did indeed lose your memories, as he suspects, then they're more likely to return to you in a matter of weeks. It's called temporary amnesia."

So, it's true, I think to myself. I did suffer from a traumatic injury that brought me to this hospital. But out of all the questions that I should ask him, there's only one inquiry that's literally rolling off my tongue.

"You're my husband?" I finally speak the words that I've been dying to ask him, ever since I opened my eyes and caught sight of him.

"My name is Senator Brent Summers," he replies, as a matter-of-fact. "And yes, I'm your husband."

Was he the same man who held my hand while I slept? I honestly don't know. But it must be. It must be him. *It has to be*. But for some reason, my heart tells me that he *isn't…*

"I'm sure that you've got a lot of questions to ask, and I promise to answer everything."

He's forward and direct. No time for nonsense. But I suppose that's perfectly normal, given that he's a politician.

At first glance, I notice that he's young and handsome, my so-called husband. He looks to be in his late thirties. Tall, slim and fit. His hair is bright blonde, like the sun, while his eyes are chocolate brown and his complexion is milky fair. And when he smiles, I notice that he has a perfectly white pair of teeth. He's the typical dashing Prince Charming-like character found from a classical fairy tale.

So, this stranger standing before me is my husband. A model-like male, who's not only handsome, but is also equally wealthy, famous and powerful, too. From what I can tell, he represents everything that most women look for in a perfect mate. Someone, whom, I've probably based all of my romantic heroes in my novels off from. And yet, when he tells me that he's my husband, I remember nothing of him. Even my heart also seems to *feel nothing* for him…

"What happened to me?" is all that I ask.

"Ah yes," he says, as he stares down at the floor. He seems nervous. "There was an accident. A hit-and-run."

"A hit-and-run?" I ask in confusion. "Was the culprit caught?"

"No, unfortunately, no," says Brent. "But the police are still investigating. All that matters is that you survived. Miraculously."

"Yes, I did," I say with much price.

Even though the world expected me to die, I simply refused.

"I know," he says with a beaming smile. "And I'm so grateful to have you back."

"So, what happens now?" I ask.

"We go home."

***

An hour later, I arrive to our home. It's a mansion located in the heart of Washington, D.C., just a few blocks away from Capitol Hill. Since my so-called husband has an office there, he made sure that we lived just a short drive away.

From what I've gathered thus far, my husband is indeed, wealthy. This mansion alone, is proof of that. In fact, this three-stories home has about twenty spare bedrooms and a staff of ten working here, full-time.

There's a grand scale library, a tennis court, a pool, a spacious ballroom, a gallery and several unoccupied offices… everything that one could ever dream or want of, it's here. This mansion is beyond anything of my comprehension. And even my own bedroom is something straight out of a modern-day fairy tale!

My bedroom alone, is a full-scale apartment. Easily, it can host a whole family of three, all on its own. Meanwhile, my closet is a home to thousands of sparkling gowns, suits, casual wear and costumes. Clothes that I've probably never even bothered to wear before. Plus, the endless racks of shoes or shelves of handbags and accessories. Capitalism at its finest.

Honestly, why do I have this much clothes, in the first place? Did I really care for them in my past life? Because right now, I don't. If all I had to wear were nothing more than a white t-shirt and a pair of blue jeans, then I'd be perfectly content with just that. But I suppose that being a senator's wife forced me to be materialistic. Because honestly, that's the only word to describe this wardrobe.

Karly Summers… who was she exactly? I can hardly remember. I'm told that she's the wife of a senator and a romance author, but these titles mean nothing to me. Or, at least the wife part. In truth, I do remember being an author. I do recall writing my novels and publishing them. I remember my fan greets and signing copies to my novels, so at least that part of my life still remains intact in my brain.

But being a wife, I remember nothing of it. Not the wedding, or the courtship, or anything else afterwards. And apparently, we've been married for the past three years. It's almost as if these past three years are a blank. But why is that? Why can't I remember?

Did Brent mean nothing to me? From what I can tell, he seems like a nice guy. Overall, he appears kind. I'm sure that I must be attracted to him. But in truth, whenever I'm around him, I don't feel that special spark. And as a romance author, I know that the *spark must* be present in every good romance. For without it, then the heroine will never succumb to her leading hero. Sparks and electricity are everything for a romantic duo.

But was Brent my romantic hero? He had to be, right? Well, for now, it doesn't matter. To Brent's credit, he's allowing me to remain alone in my own bedroom. Furthermore, he promises not to make any physical advancements towards me. At least, not until I'm ready.

For now, as I stand outside on my private balcony overlooking the scenic city view, I'm happily content in this moment. At present, I am grateful. Earlier this morning, I was at death's door and now, I'm standing back up on my own two feet.

Even though Brent claims that my accident was due to an unplanned hit-and-run, but either way, I'm suspicious. Unfortunately, I don't agree with him. In truth, I don't believe that my accident was random or unplanned. No, I don't believe that, not for one second. Someone wanted me dead. That much I do know. That much I can *remember*. But who that was and why, still remains to be seen.

One way or another, I'm not safe until I get to the bottom of this mystery. After all, my own life depends upon it.

CHAPTER 3

Crystal Blue Eyes

The next morning, I head downstairs for breakfast, where I meet Brent's brother. Well, stepbrother to be technically correct. No, actually, he's his *former stepbrother*. Their parents have since divorced.

"Honey, do you remember Jake?" Brent asks me point blank.

As I take my seat, I stare across the dining room table and take a good solid look at him. This man is by far, the handsomest man that I've ever laid my eyes upon. His hair is jet black, like a raven. His eyes crystal blue, like the deep sea. His features are sharp and well refined. Almost regal. Plus, his demeanor is suave and sophisticated. Meanwhile, he's dressed in a navy-blue suit, with a white blouse and a black tie. He's a professional, to be sure. In fact, he looks to be around Brent's age. Could he be another politician, like Brent?

As I stare into his face, I can see the anticipation in his eyes. It's squinted and focused. He's anxious, for those blue irises of his are illuminated. They're shining and sparkling, just like a rare gem. It's almost sapphire blue now in color.

He *wants* me to remember. That much I can tell. Feel. This

man… Jake… is his name… his eyes speak a thousand unspoken words. This man *knows me* and he *desperately* wants me to remember him. To remember something about my past...

Except, I don't. I can't. No matter how much he wants me to, or how much *I* want to, I just can't remember him. No memories. Nothing. But unlike Brent, I do *feel* like I know him… like I was *supposed* to know him… like I *did* know him…

A second later, I blink. Somehow, I got lost in the moment. Instantly, I look away and stare down at the floor.

"I'm sorry… I just don't…"

I lift my head back up and revert my gaze towards him, again. To my horror, I instantly see the anguish and despair written across on his face. He is *devastated.* But yet, he admits nothing. Instead, he remains absolutely silent. His body might be stiff and proper, but his own eyes betray him…

Amazingly enough, even Brent doesn't take any notice about Jake's odd reaction. In fact, come to think of it, Brent didn't react in this same way, when I failed to recognize him. Brent might not have cared about my lack of memories concerning him, but Jake certainly does. Because in his eyes, I can see it all, reflected most clearly. He, unlike Brent, cares.

I might not know Jake or Brent or myself, for that matter. But this much I do know: I *meant* something to this man. And from the looks of it, I *still* do matter. But why? How? How can a total stranger like Jake— someone who's *supposed* to be my so-called husband's stepbrother— care so much for me?

The irony of it all, is that I know absolutely nothing about this man; but yet, I'm strangely attracted to him at the same time, too. He feels oddly familiar and deep down inside, I know that he was important to me. My memories might be lost, but my heart still beats for this stranger.

"It's quite alright," Brent replies on Jake's behalf. "This is Jake Valliant, my former stepbrother. My mother used to be married to his father back in the day."

"Oh, so I see," is all that I can say.

Instantly, Jake's blue eyes meet my own hazel eyes and almost immediately, I feel a sudden spark go down my back. A moment later, my heart begins to rapidly race and for some odd reason, I long to rush straight into his arms. His stare is so incredibly intense, that lakes could freeze with just one look at his powerful gaze. Jake might be silent, but his unspoken words say so much. He is angry, that much I can tell. But more than anything, he is also *hurt*…

"Don't think too much of it," Brent shrugs, nonchalant. "I'm sure you'll remember Jake, eventually. In fact, I'll bet that once you remember me, then you'll probably recall him, too. After all, we used to joke that you were married to the both of us."

"Come again?" my ears go up. Why on earth, would anyone say that? I, Karly Summers, married to two men at the same time?

But instead of answering my question, Brent laughs on. Meanwhile, Jake remains as silent as ever.

A few seconds later, Brent's laughter dies down and he tells me, "I might be your husband in name, but Jake over here, now he's always been your to-go guy. Your right-hand man. Well technically, both our right-hand man."

"I'm not following…" I utter.

"I'm an attorney," Jake finally speaks, breaking his prolonged silence.

It's the first time that I've heard him speak, and his voice is deep and as sharp and as calm as ever.

"Not only is he our attorney," Brent chimes in, "But he's also our fixer upper. Jake takes care of everything for us. Public relations, accounting, booking, he does everything. At all hours of the day. Have a scandal or a crisis with the press? He's on our speed dial. Or hungry for a late-night snack? I'll call him, before I contact Door-Dash. Jake is our guy."

"So, you might be my husband in name, but Jake is my true confident?" I finally ask.

"Yes," Jake replies, this time. "I am and have always been, your trusted friend."

"And that he is," Brent adds on. "That's why I say, I might be your husband in name, but in spirit, Jake's your mate."

Is that why he feels so familiar to me? Jake was my best friend? But why would a married woman need to have another best friend, apart from her husband? Just what sort of marriage did I have with Brent?

"I see," is all that I say.

A few minutes later, I proceed to eat my bowl of oatmeal, as Brent and Jake finish the rest of their pancakes. Afterwards, both men excuse themselves from the table and head off to work.

From what I've gathered during breakfast, Jake often visits Brent daily to give him a run-down of his morning schedule. And even though he has a room reserved within this mansion, Jake seldomly uses it. Instead, he owns his own apartment in downtown. Apparently, he's single and has never been married.

As a married woman, I know that I shouldn't care about his single status. But the truth is, that I do. I do care. In fact, I'm delighted that he's single.

As it currently stands, I feel absolutely nothing for Brent. Whether he's kind or not, I still feel nothing towards him. No attraction. No attachment. Not even a sliver of curiosity directed towards him, nor our past. Although I might be married to him right now, but do I *still want* to be married to him in the future?

A part of me feels obligated to stay with him. After all, the old Karly married him. Therefore, I must have *loved* him at some point. However, if I were to divorce him now, then what does that say about me? That I'm the type of person, who gives up so easily in a marriage? That I'm betraying my old self by turning my back on a husband, that I can't even remember? And even if I do remember him, then will I also remember loving him, too?

Because at this moment, one thing remains perfectly clear: I'm not in love with my husband. This is, and was, a loveless marriage; at least, from my perspective. Whether or not Brent truly loves me or not, that still remains to be seen.

But as I wander off back onto my balcony and stare out across the clear blue sky, all I can think about is Jake. How blue his eyes are, just like this sky. *Crystal blue eyes.* How much he longed for me to remember him. To be fair, even Brent didn't have that same look of longing in his eyes. But with Jake, it's different.

This stranger cares about me. He might not be my husband, but in my heart, I already know that this fact alone doesn't matter. And as I close my eyes shut, I imagine his thick lips pressed against mine. Meanwhile, as he holds me tight within his embrace, the smell of his cologne sends me into a daze.

Instantly, I reopen my eyes. Fantasizing about a man, while I'm still married to another, along with a ring around my finger, it's supposed to be wrong. I should feel guilty. But in truth, I don't. Instead, I feel… well… *happy*…

And happiness with a man who's supposed to be my husband's stepbrother (or former stepbrother) is nothing else short but… *dangerous!*

CHAPTER 4

Red Roses

Two days later, I joined Brent to attend a luxurious state dinner held at the prestigious and exclusive Waldorf Astoria Hotel in downtown D.C., for a night of celebration. The who's who from Capitol Hill are all here, in attendance. Senators, congress representatives, judges, clerks, lawyers, doctors, scientists, engineers, journalists, lobbyists, wall street businessmen, billionaires, entrepreneurs, executives, students, interns, administrators and everyone else that's a part of the grand world of American politics. Tonight, they're all here. And in a banquet room filled with hundreds of wealthy and ambitious elites, I couldn't possibly feel more out of place.

Just how did a romance novelist, like myself, end up married to an American Senator? According to Brent, we met three years ago in Los Angeles (my hometown) and the rest was history. Apparently, we were staying at the same hotel. While he was busy mingling with other businessmen at the bar, I was promoting one of my latest book releases in the next conference room over. And by pure luck, we just so happened to accidentally bump into each other at the lobby. According to him, we instantly hit-it-right-off. And a few weeks later, we married and my life has been a rom-com ever since...

Except, I highly doubt that. In fact, I know that my life *isn't* a rom-com, it's never been. Because, in truth, it feels so far from it. No, my life is more like a thriller. Especially, given my current amnesiac status…

But apart from all of this, I also find it highly odd for him to say that we hit-it-right-off, given that I seem to have absolutely nothing in common with my husband, as of right now. After spending these past two days in his company, I can safely conclude that Brent and I are two very different people with very little to no similarities.

Apart from his job, Brent prefers playing video games, reading comic books and drinking beer in his private study; whereas, I'm usually reading novels or wandering off for a stroll through the garden. I know that most married couples have their own separate hobbies; but still, I find it rather strange that out of all the people to be married to in this world, I somehow ended up with Brent. And I don't even care for politics... or at least… I think I don't…

I should feel guilty for not trying to see past his faults, but I can't help myself. But in honor of my past self, I've decided to humor old Karly. Old Karly must have loved Brent. And so, in her honor, I've accepted Brent's invitation to attend tonight's state dinner.

And so, for the past hour, I've remained seated beside Brent and sporting a disingenuous smile upon my face. As it turns out, Brent is a popular senator. He practically knows everyone from the D.C. area. But that isn't so surprising, given the fact that he's a senator elected from this region. However, people genuinely seem to like him. Including his staff, his fellow senators on both sides of the aisle, and a few other notable billionaires and entrepreneurs.

I should be impressed, but I'm neutral. Still, even by me mingling with all of these people, I can't remember them. I can't recall not a single face. It's like the past three years have been completely wiped away from my brain. Honestly, I wonder as to why that is.

Apparently, my accident made headlines. And so, just about everyone here at this event has not only given me their condolences, but many of them are truly astonished that I actually survived the ordeal. In truth, it really was a miracle.

Not only was I in a coma for two whole months, but I also experienced a severe concussion, as well as several bruising across my body. Luckily, most of my injuries have since healed; with the exception to a bad black and blue bruise still lingering across on my stomach. But apart from this, I was blessed not to have sustained any broken bones or other internal injuries. Well, apart from my memories…

But as I shake hands with the politicians and their spouses, along with the other billionaires, entrepreneurs, doctors, judges and all of the rest, I can't help but wonder if anyone of these people might be the mysterious driver who was behind the wheel on that fateful day of my accident. Is it possible that someone, here in this very room, is the same person who ran over me? Was it someone that I once knew, or was it truly a total stranger? After all, the police still haven't caught the culprit, so anything is possible.

I'm not a detective and as an author, I've never written a mystery or a thriller before. But for the first in my life, I wish I had. Perhaps, if I had written one, then maybe, just maybe, I'd be capable enough to solve my own case. Because as it stands, someone wanted me dead. That much I do *remember*.

After finishing the main course, I decide to step outside to get some much-needed fresh air. However, before I do, Brent promptly grabs a hold of my hand. It's the first time that he's touched me, since my return back from the hospital. But instead of feeling butterflies in my stomach, to my own surprise, I'm repulsed by his touch. Not matter how handsome he might look; I still feel no spark of attraction towards him. But in an effort not to offend him, I keep a smiling face and allow him to hold my hand. And then, before I know it, he escorts me over to the dance floor.

Have I ever danced before? Can I even dance, in the first place? Honestly, I don't remember. However, Brent senses my hesitation and quickly seeks to reassure me.

"Don't worry, just follow my lead," he tells me.

Thus far, Brent is kind, patient and lighthearted. He smiles a lot, I notice. I also notice that he catches the eyes of several women, too. Especially, at this party. But I'm not a jealous wife. In order to be jealous, one must care for one's spouse. And thus far, I'm deeply failing in this department.

As the music begins to play, Brent's arm wraps tightly around my waist, hooking to the black sequins in my gown. Slowly, we begin to move and as promised, I follow his lead.

Standing this close to Brent, I immediately catch a whiff of his cologne. It's strong and smells a lot like lemons with a hint of honey. It's a fresh and sweet aroma and for some reason, I'm not at all surprised that it's his signature scent.

Apart from being a politician, at his core, Brent is a simple and cheerful man. A former college footballer who accidentally fell into the world of politics. Mainly due to his own biological father's ongoing persistence. After all, Brent's father was a former mayor himself, stemming from a small city in the state of Wisconsin.

But even being around Brent in this close proximately, doesn't trigger anything for me. Although I wonder how it must feel for him to be so close to me. Does Brent miss me? Me, specifically, acting as his wife? Does he miss kissing me? Holding me? Making love to me? After all, he's still a young man, so it would only be natural to lust after one's wife.

Even though Brent promised to behave, I still often wonder on how long that promise will truly last. What if my memories never return? What if I never remember my love for him? Will he still be okay with that reality? Will *I* be okay with that sort of future?

"Anything coming back to you, honey?" he whispers into my ear.

Sadly, no. Absolutely, nothing comes to my mind. Dancing with either him or a total stranger, makes no difference at all. I still feel nothing. I still remember nothing.

"No, I'm sorry," I whisper back to him.

"It okay," he sighs. "Eventually, you will."

"You know," he continues on, "I'm wearing this red rose in my pocket, as a corsage in your honor."

"Really? Why?"

"Why, red roses are your favorite. That's why. Don't you at least remember that?"

Again, complete blankness. No, I don't recall the red rose as being my favorite flower. I should, but I don't. But even though Brent claims that it is, my heart tells me that it *isn't*…

And then, to my surprise he places a light kiss above my forehead. It's sweet, tender and innocent. Almost like a simple peck on the cheek. But most importantly, it's done right in front of this huge crowd, that's currently watching us dance. And because of this mere fact alone, I can't help but wonder if Brent really wanted to kiss me because he truly wanted to, or did he do it on purpose to humor the standing crowd before us? Either way, I can't help but wonder…

Suddenly, the music stops playing and Brent escorts me back to our seats. But along the way, we bump into a young woman. She's wearing a red strapless dress, that's form fitted against the curves of her slim figure. It's an outfit, that ironically, resembles a real-life scarlet rose come straight into life.

Furthermore, this young female has short and curly blonde hair, bright blue eyes, of medium height and sports a sweet smile. She looks rather young, too. Perhaps, she's in her mid-twenties? Maybe, she's an intern?

"Honey, this is my assistant," says Brent. "Do you remember her? This is Abigail Rose."

Abigail Rose… that name sounds so familiar. I've heard it before. And then, I catch a second glimpse of her face and then…

Suddenly, I can't breathe. This is odd. There's a tightness in my chest. And now, I'm finding it difficult to gasp for air. Am I nervous? Anxious? And if so, then why?

"Honey, are you okay?" Brent asks, as he catches a hold of my arm.

"I'm fine," I quickly say. "I think I just need some air."

"Would you like for me to escort you outside?" Abigail asks, this time.

"No!" I shout at the top of my lungs. Honestly, what has come over me to yell like this at a total stranger?

And my reaction certainly doesn't go unnoticed. Instantly, Brent and Abigail are taken aback by my harsh outburst.

"I'm sorry, it's the crowd… I need space…"

And before I even finish my sentence, I immediately take off. Running down the hallway as fast as I possibly can, while desperately searching for an exit. Anything to get some fresh air. Anything to *escape*.

After running down to the end of this hallway, I finally discover a door. As I open it, I suddenly lose my balance. One way or another, I'm about to tumble straight down…

Except that I don't. Instead, someone catches me mid-air. And now, someone is holding me. And tightly, too. Being in the dark corner of the hallway, I can't see them. But I can smell them. It's a woodsy and pine scent. An intoxicating male scent that I absolutely adore.

Instantly, his large hands tightly grip mine. And with little to no effort on his part, he gently lifts me back up to stand on my own two feet. And now, he's standing right behind me, that much I know. That much I can *feel*. And whomever he is, he certainly saved me from a disastrous fall. But before I can turn around to thank him, he suddenly speaks to me.

"Keep your eyes focus at all times," he warns. "And don't trust anyone, *darling*."

For a second, my heart skips a beat. *Darling*. It's *him*. The man who watched over me at the hospital. My guardian angel. My savior.

Instantly, I turn around. But to my great disappointment, he's disappeared. Vanished into thin air. Sadly, my mystery hero is long *gone*.

Afterwards, I revert my gaze back towards the party at the end of the hall. From this view, I can see Brent, along with his assistant, busy mingling with the other guests. And finally, with much clarity, I see the truth. Well, at least, I see a part of the truth.

My mystery man is *not* my husband. This stranger is someone *else*. But who my savior is, still remains to be seen.

In the meantime, I need to take his advice to heart. I do need to pay a better attention to my surroundings. And most importantly, trust no one. Including my husband.

CHAPTER 5

White Roses

A week later, I find myself seated in the library and reviewing a stack of my old books. As it turns out, I'm not only a romance author, but I also specialize in historical romances, too. Mostly, my novels are set during the Regency Era, with my heroes generally portrayed by dukes, earls and other high nobles. And by the way, Jane Austen, is my favorite author to date!

Do I remember writing these novels? Actually, yes, surprisingly, I do! I remember everything about my career. Every story, every novel… every written word. At least that part of my life still remains perfectly intact in my memories. Something constant in my brain.

But in truth, I actually remember almost everything about my past, too. My childhood, my parents, my friends, my college years and my career. Almost everything… with the exception to these last three years.

I can remember everything up until *then*. Afterwards, it's a complete blur. A black out. For some reason, these last three years' worth of memories simply vanished into thin air. Which coincidentally, corresponds to the length of my marriage…

With regards to my marriage as a whole, still, I recall almost *nothing*. It's odd how I can't remember this part of my life. Not a single memory of being with Brent or our lives spent together. I should remember it, but yet, I can't…

According to my doctor, Dr. Hakim Khan, this is normal. For some reason, I'm blocking my time spent with Brent. Dr. Khan believes that it might be attributed to some sort of trauma, but what kind of trauma could it possibly be?

From the looks of it, Brent *seems* like a nice guy. As of yet, he hasn't been cruel or unpleasant towards me. Our lives together are supposed to be the perfect fairy tale marriage. A woman married to a modern-day Prince Charming. A wealthy American Senator. But yet, I fail to remember Brent as Prince Charming. In fact, at present, I fail to find anything charming about him at all. But then again, what do I really know of Brent? After all, my husband is a stranger to me. Charming or not.

And in truth, I hardly see Brent. Between our busy schedules, he's often at work. And when he's not at work, he frequently travels. Most of the time, I find myself alone at the mansion. But ironically, this actually works to my favor.

With Brent gone, I spend most of my days at the library. My unofficial office, where I've been using this time to write. In fact, my current story is about the Duke of Cornwall falling for a young widow, named Karoline, the Countess of Mulberry. Jacob, the Duke of Cornwall, silently loves my heroine. He's loved her since forever. Even before her marriage to the earl. And yet, the duke remains silent. He's fearful to confess his true feelings to her. He's afraid that if he does, then he will risk losing their friendship…

And ironically, the duke resembles Jake so much. The same dark hair, crystal blue eyes, fair skin and powerful smile. Was I inspired by him, when I first started writing this manuscript prior to my accident? It's uncanny how much the duke and Jake are similar, both in appearances and in personality.

But shouldn't Brent have served as the true inspiration to my romantic heroes in my novels? From what I've read thus far, no, I don't believe so. Karly of yesterday cared about Jake. This much I do *know* from the bottom of my heart. Of my soul. My old self adored this man so much, that she even wrote him into one of her books!

The story is still unfinished and so, I'm determined to write the ending. But how should I end it? Give my heroine a happily ever after? Reunite Jacob with Karoline? What about my own life? What about my own happily ever after?

Luckily, I'm left alone in this library with nothing else but my silent thoughts. Honestly, I enjoy being alone. I relish in solitude. At least this way, by writing again, perhaps, a regular routine will help me to remember. Recall the woman that I once was, prior to my accident.

But unfortunately, I've spoken too soon. Because at this very moment, the doors have flung wide open and behold, my real-life duke has just walked through them. It's Jake Valliant, in the flesh.

"Good afternoon, Karly," he says, as he walks over to a bookshelf across from me.

"Good afternoon, Jake," I reply. "Business in the library?"

"Always," Jake smiles back at me, as he retrieves a heavy encyclopedia from off the shelf.

A second later, he pulls out a chair and takes a seat right next to me at the table. But instead of having a direct conversation with me, he remains absolutely silent. It's almost as if, he respects my work. He must know that I'm currently busy typing away on my latest novel. And rather than disturbing me, he's silently reading his book. And as I stare at him from the corner of my eye, I notice a faint smile appear on the side of his face. He's secretly happy to be near me. Without saying not, a single word, and already, I can instantly tell that I've just made his whole day. No… his entire week.

One way or another, this man genuinely cares for me. *Loves me.* I can simply *feel* it. Penetrating right down to my very bones. At my core. He doesn't have to speak those three precious words aloud, but already, I know the *truth*.

From his silent gestures to his genuine smile, I see it all. And so far, he's never smiled like this before. Not even to Brent or anyone else at the mansion. For all his worth, Jake is a quiet, respectful and a well-reserved man. Generally, he keeps to himself and always acts ever-so proper. However, whenever it comes to me, that's when his crystal blue eyes finally light up. It shines so brightly, just for me.

"Anything of importance?" I finally ask him, breaking our prolonged silence.

"Just another law book," he answers, with another deep smile. A smile that beams like the moon. Instantly, my heart skips a beat.

"Ah, yes," I say, blushingly. "You're a lawyer. Naturally, you'd be reading law books."

"Yes, naturally," Jake replies, with that gorgeous smile of his. "Actually, Brent is considering a new bill to increase funding at the local D.C. public schools."

"Oh, that's wonderful!" I happily exclaim. For the first time since returning back home, I'm actually interested in Brent's job. Geez, politics, who knew!

Jakes smiles again and says, "Yes, I knew you'd be. It's why I'm researching it, in the first place."

"What do you mean?" I ask in surprise.

"The subject of education has always been important to you," he tells me. "Particularly, in the field of writing."

"Ah, the writing part," I say. "No wonder. Even without my memories, I still know that's important to me. Educating young minds are essential and…"

"Can make a world of a difference," he interjects.

Instantly, I smile back at him. That's right. That's exactly what I was going to say. Somehow, one way or another, Jake can finish my own sentences. Right down to the very words.

"You know me rather well, don't you?"

"Yes," he's quick to say. "I do know you rather well. Perhaps, best of all."

Almost immediately, I am lost for words. He's caught me off guard. Jakes knows me through and through. Far better than my own husband. And this fact alone, terrifies me.

Without thinking any further, I stand up and walk over to across the room. I'm now standing by the front entrance table and gazing down at a bouquet of white roses. The smell is absolutely divine. It's fresh, sweet and light. Brent might have claimed that the red rose was my favorite flower. However, while gazing down at these exquisite white roses, I can't help but think differently.

"You know," I begin to tell Jake, "Brent claims that the red rose is my favorite flower, but gazing down at these lovely white roses, I can't help but feel that isn't quite true. Red might be a popular choice, but white is much more elegant. Serene. Loving. Liberating. Free."

"Well, that's silly," Jake says, as he rises up from his chair and walks over to my side.

Ten steps later, he's standing right behind me. I can feel his body, pressed up behind mine. I can even hear him gently breathing down my neck. Meanwhile, his cologne is rugged and woodsy. I absolutely adore it. Having him stand so close to me, feels *so incredibly good.*

"Of course, you don't care for red roses," he whispers gently into my ear, using his velvet and seductive voice. "White roses have *always* been your favorite. That's why I frequently keep a bouquet for you in this very library at all times. It's here, just for *you*."

And then, suddenly, a *memory* reappears in my mind. I recall standing right here, in this very spot and gazing into Jake's crystal blue eyes, while I happily smile at him. He's standing in front of me, while holding a bouquet of white roses, along with a blue ribbon wrapped around it. Graciously, he offers his bouquet over to me and as I take them, he slowly leans in and…

Instantly, I'm jolted right back to the present. This is my first and only memory of my past. And it's with Jake, of all people. This can't be a coincidence. My memories with this man, they matter. He was, and still is, important to me. And in that memory, did… we… *almost kiss?*

"Are you okay," Jake asks, as he catches me in his arms. Apparently, I might have slipped out of consciousness for a brief minute. But already, the feel of his arms around me… feels so…

"I think… I think I might have had a memory…" I utter. "And it was with… *you*."

Much to my surprise, he smiles from ear to ear, as he brings me back to stand on my own two feet. He's delighted to hear about this new revelation. For once, Jake looks genuinely thrilled. And his blissful mirth is shining right through his bright blue eyes. Honestly, his joy is contagious, because I'm equally thrilled, too.

"You're finally coming back to me, Karly," he tells me.

Perhaps, I am. Maybe, I am coming back. Maybe, soon enough, I'll remember everything once again. Hopefully.

And then, to my surprise, he gives me a hug. It's something that's he's longed to do, that much I can feel from his embrace. And as his heart beats against mine, I realize that although I might not remember him in full, it still doesn't change how I feel about him, right now. How hard my heart flutters for him, at this very second.

This hug feels so familiar. And even as a stranger, I know… I just *know*… that deep down inside… hidden within the secret chambers of my heart… that… I *still love* this man, either way. Yes, *I love* Jake Valliant. Karly Summers *loves* Jake Valliant. And somehow, in this sick and twisted universe, Jake Valliant *loves* Karly Summers, in return.

Slowly, Jake pulls himself from my embrace and briefly walks away. A second later, he returns to my side, gently pushes my brown hair aside and tucks a single white rose bud behind my ear. Again, his touch, it feels magical. Just the simple brush of his hand against my skin and already, I feel undone.

"Remember," he says, "Brent might be your husband. But you and me, we're soul mates."

And then, Jake leans in and gives me a tender kiss alongside my forehead. While Brent's kiss might have been brief and no more than a simple peck; however, Jake's kiss lingers on. Overall, his kiss feels more caring and heartfelt. Almost *loving*.

But before I have a chance to react, he abruptly pulls away from me and then exits the library. Meanwhile, I'm left standing behind, with my hand held over my chest. Over my beating heart that *yearns* for this man, full memories or not.

In the end, my mind might not recognize him, but my heart certainly, does.

CHAPTER 6

A View at Capitol Hill

A week later, I receive a call from Brent's assistant, Abigail Rose, with a lunch invitation, curtesy of my husband. Since it's been a week to the date as to when I last saw him, I decided to accept her offer. After all, he's been recently traveling throughout the east coast and it's the least that I can do. If he wants to have lunch with me, then I shouldn't deny him this simple request.

But for some reason, I don't like this, Abigail Rose. Why that is, I'm not entirely certain. Thus far, she hasn't been cruel or unkind to me. But either way, the sound of her voice and her over well-being, it just rubs off on me in the wrong sort of way. Is it possible that the old Karly didn't like her in the past, either? And for good reason, too?

Regardless, it hardly matters. Whether or not the past version of myself liked her or not, it's of little to no consequences to me, now. Abigail Rose is Brent's assistant and that's that. His career is none of my business, just like my books are none of his.

And so, on one fine Tuesday afternoon, I change into a plain black dress, slip on a pair of brown flats, grab my black leather handbag and then, I hop into a taxi headed straight to Capitol Hill.

As I walk into the building, to my unexpected surprise, I encounter a second memory. I've walked down this hallway before. I've seen these marble steps. And as I approach the door to Brent's office, I see Abigail seated in her chair. She's laughing at me. Mocking me. Cursing at me...

Suddenly, I'm jolted back to the present. That was strange. It was a second memory. I remember Abigail, but not on good terms. Why was she laughing at me? Mocking me? Cursing at me? I, the wife of her boss?

Finally, I reach Brent's door and push it open. At first glance, his workspace is empty. It's noon time and no one's around. No staff or interns. No one.

Curiously, I decide to walk further in to his office's department. It's a large white wing that's covered in navy-blue carpet all around the floors, along with several rows of secretarial coffee brown desks placed strategically in front of each of his staffers' offices' doors. Additionally, there's an oversized American flag on a pole that's displayed right in the center, near an exit. Overall, it's a typical and uniformed office space designated for a U.S. Senator.

I'm tempted to turn around and leave. Obviously, Brent must have forgotten about our lunch appointment. However, before I take another step back, I suddenly hear noises coming from the next room over.

The sounds are that of a man and a woman, giggling. They're having a good time. Even though I know that it's none of my business; but still, I'm curious. Who are they and why are they laughing in a place of business? In my husband's office? And a public office, at that?

And so, I walk towards the door and gently push it open. And to my surprise, I uncover yet another layer of mystery to my forgotten past.

There before me, is my husband, lying stark naked above his assistant, Abigail Rose. Also, equally naked. Like Adam and Eve, they're lying above on his office desk and making love to each other, right before my eyes.

So, Brent was never faithful to me, was he? No wonder, I've felt cold towards him from the very beginning. My mind might not remember the truth, but my heart still does. My heart has always known. It still remembers his betrayal. Then *and* now.

Again, they're laughing, as he kisses her till kingdom come. Meanwhile, they're lying above a bed of roses, with red petals scattered everywhere. If red roses had indeed been my favorite in the past, then Brent truly exploited it.

Rather than confronting him, I decide to leave. Brent might be my husband in name, but he's still a stranger to me. His betrayal doesn't hit as hard to me, because in truth, I hardly know him. Therefore, I don't care about his scandalous affair, as much as I probably should.

A few minutes later, I find myself seated down on a wooden bench outside of Brent's building, underneath a cherry blossom tree and pondering about my future. I might not remember about my past, but this much I do know: Karly, of today, doesn't want this sort of life. No, Karly, as of right now, doesn't want to stay married to a cheating senator, no matter how rich or famous he might be. Prince Charming or not.

And then, it suddenly becomes crystal clear. I was given a second chance in this life. A second blessing to undue all the wrongs of my past. Just because I married Brent, doesn't mean that I have to remain married to him. I can move on. Rebuild my life from scratch again, without him.

With a new sense of pride, I gaze down at the ground and ironically, I notice a single red rose petal laying there. Jake was right, red roses aren't my favorite flower at all. In fact, I *loathe* them.

Without a further thought, I trample over that rose petal and crush it into pieces. Turning it into nothing more than dust. Destroying what was never really mine to begin with.

A few minutes later, I decide to reward myself. And so, I buy myself a fresh bouquet of white roses at the nearby corner flower stand. Afterwards, I head for home to pack a suitcase.

This time around, Karly Summers is going to live life to the fullest. At long last, Karly Summers is going to finally have a happily ever after!

CHAPTER 7

This Isn't My Life (That I Want!)

An hour later, I'm back at the mansion and packing a suitcase. I have no idea where I'm heading to, or how my life will be from here on out. But this much I do know: my marriage is *over*. I will divorce Brent, if it's the last thing that I do.

No matter my past, I refuse to stay married in the present to an unfaithful husband. This isn't my life… or at least… the sort of life that I want to lead. I don't want an open marriage. I don't want an unfaithful husband. I don't want to share a husband. Instead, I want a husband who loves me for me, and only me. No exceptions.

And if I'm being perfectly honest, I do want children. I'm still young and I know that with the right person by my side, I can eventually have them. But either way, I can't picture Brent being the father of my future children. I refuse to bring children into this world, only to have him be their father. No, hell would have to freeze over before I'd ever allow for that to happen!

I'm not particularly attached to anything in this mansion, so I pack a rather light suitcase. Just enough clothes to get me by for the next few days, until I figure things out.

Should I return back to Los Angeles? After all, it's where I'm originally from. Where my parents still reside. Plus, as I do recall, I have a sister there, too. Marissa and her husband, Jason.

Or, if not my parents or sister, then perhaps, I can stay with my cousin in New York, instead. That's even closer to D.C. My cousin, Dr. Kate Stanley. She's a professor at New York University. And ironically, she, like me, also married a government official. Except, her husband is an ambassador. Perhaps, I could stay with either Kate or Marissa?

As I close up my suitcase, a hear a knock at my door. Without answering, the door immediately swings right open. Behold, Jake has entered into my bedroom.

"I'm leaving," I flat out tell him.

"I know," he replies. "It's why I've come."

"How did… you… know?" I ask in surprise.

"I always know, whenever it comes to you," he sighs. "Come on, let's go."

And before I know it, he's holding my suitcase on his left hand and his right hand is intertwined with mine.

"Where are you taking me?"

"Away from here."

"Which is?"

"My apartment."

Instantly, my heart drops to my stomach. Alone with Jake, in his apartment? Just him and me? The temptation is far too great!

"What's wrong?" he turns around to ask me, face-to-face. His eyes as crystal blue as ever.

"I… I…" but I don't have anything to say to him.

The truth is that I'm *afraid* to be alone with him. And yet, I also *desperately want* to be alone with him, too. All at the same exact time.

And if I'm being perfectly honest to myself, it's more than just being alone with Jake. Instead, I want to lie naked with him in his bed. To have his strong arms wrapped tightly around my waist, as he passionately kisses me until judgment day. I want to be *his*, and for him to be *mine*. But is this wishful dream, even remotely possible? After all, he's Brent's stepbrother. Correction: *former* stepbrother.

"What about Brent?" I ask him point blank.

"What about him?" he asks me in return.

"Aren't you loyal to him first, before me?" I finally ask the million-dollar question.

"No," he growls, underneath his breath. Instantly, my words have upset him.

"I am," he continues, "Loyal to one and only one person. And in case you're wondering, that's you, Karly."

And before I know it, he pulls me into his chest and kisses the top of my head. Never in my life, have I ever felt so protected.

"Anyone who hurts you or makes you cry, is an enemy of mine," he fiercely proclaims. "You are all that matters. You're my Karly. Always have and always will be."

To my surprise, he lifts me up into his arms and carries me away. And just like that, me and my suitcase are off to his apartment. Jake, my true knight in shining armor. My real-life duke.

CHAPTER 8

The Duke of My Heart

A few hours later, I find myself alone in Jake's apartment. Like Brent, he's also rich, too. Apparently, his father is a wealthy Texan oil tycoon from Dallas. Jake's family comes from old money. Brent's mother was his father's third wife. And even though his father married at least three more times since (for a grand total of six marriages and counting), Jake is his only child… as well as his sole heir to his grand fortune and estates…

Not that this fact matters to me in the very least. Poor or rich, I truly don't care. I'd gladly take Jake's company over the King of England. Over a real-life duke. Sometimes in life, money isn't everything. Not a single penny is worth selling your soul for it. In truth, it's the wealth of love and friendship that counts the most.

But from what I can tell, Jake has an exquisite apartment, that resembles more of an upscale penthouse. It's located on the top floor of a ten-stories building, in the heart of downtown and overlooks the city view. Apart from the master's bedroom, there's four spare bedrooms, plus two additional bathrooms and an oversized balcony. Plus, it's also walking distance from the mansion, but still far away enough to give me some-much needed privacy and time. Time away to rest and to strategize the rest of my life, from here on out.

"I know a few good divorce attorneys in the city, who can handle your case. In fact, my friend, Blake Everett, can easily have your case settled in less than a month," he tells me, as he takes a seat by the sofa next to me and hands me a cup of Earl of Grey tea, with a dash of milk. Apparently, it's my favorite.

"That's helpful, thank you," I say, as I take a sip of my tea.

Heavens, this tea *is* good. Somehow, everything that Jake touches turns into gold. It's amazing how one man can know me so much. Even better than how I know myself.

"Enjoying the tea?" Jake asks with a beaming smile. Already, he can tell from my reaction, just how much I adore it, too.

"Yes, how did you know?"

"The right side of your lip curves up, whenever you like something," he says and then blushes.

Dear God, this man *really does* know it all. Amazing.

"I wish I knew you, as much as you know about me," I admit to him in shame. Good or bad, it is the honest truth.

"In time, you will," he says. "*Again.*"

"Jake," I take a bold risk and ask him directly, "In the past, we're we… we… *lovers?*"

"Not one to overlook anything, aren't you?" he teases me.

But based on his reaction, I can't help but think that *yes*, I am correct. Jake was my lover. He had to be.

"Yes and no," he replies.

"Really, how so?" I press on.

"First of all," he begins, "You're not one to cheat. Regardless of Brent's extramarital affairs, you've held on to your honor. It's why I admire you so damn much."

"So, him and Abigail, this isn't Brent's first affair, is it?" I ask. By now, I already told him everything that I saw back at Capitol Hill.

"No, it's not," Jake sighs. "Unfortunately, Brent acquired this straying trait from my own dear father. No matter the circumstances, he just can't keep his pants on. Not even, for a single day."

"Did I try to divorce him in the past?" I inquire. Really, I just have to know.

But instead of answering my question, he asks me, "Can you really not remember?"

Somewhere, hidden within the depths of my mind, lies the answer. Although my mind still doesn't remember the whole truth; however, my heart does. My heart knows that Brent and I were going to divorce. But somewhere along the way, something happened…

"I still can't recall," I shake my head. "But in my heart, I know that we're not meant to be. I know that I must have wanted to divorce him. Because me, the Karly right now, can't stand to even look at him. Therefore, I must have wanted to divorce him. But what stopped me?"

"It was the accident," he reveals, with a heavy heart.

"What?" I choke. "Was I about to divorce him, before I fell into a coma?"

Without saying another word, he nods and there is my long-awaited answer. I was going to divorce Brent, after all. And if I divorced Brent, then that means, I was going to be with…

"I was going to divorce Brent to be with you, wasn't I?"

"Yes," he whispers.

And then, I look at him. Really look at him. There's a tear in his eye, like I've finally captured his heart. This man has been suffering. Silently, he's been in pain. He's been desperately waiting for me to remember. To remember *him*.

But even though I fail to remember my past, I realize that it no longer matters. Because memories or not, I *love* this man. And more importantly, I *want* to be with him. I want this honest and kind-hearted man to be the father of my children. I want him to be by my constant side. I want to live the rest of my life here on this earth, with him. Just him and me. *Together.*

"I might not remember you," I say, as I open up my heart to him, "But it doesn't matter. All my heroes in my novels, they're based on you. The dukes, the earls and the wealthy lords from my stories, they're all based on you, Jake, the duke of my heart. That much, I know. Memories or not, either way, I love you, Jake. The Karly then and the Karly now, still wants you. She still craves for your touch. And everything else that lovers do. Now, and forever."

Instantly, he leaps up from the sofa and scoops me straight into his arms. Alas, I've said the magic words. Tenderly and affectionately, he cradles me near his warm chest. Meanwhile, as he brushes my hair aside, he leans his head above my head. And after all this time, I've never felt more at home.

"I can't tell you how much you mean to me," he confesses. "I'd give up my life for yours in an instant. You and I are meant to be."

Happiness quickly overwhelms me. Instantly, I begin to cry. But they're not tears of sadness, but of joy. For the first time since awakening from my coma, I am truly happy. Blissfully over the moon.

"Shush," he tells me as he holds me tightly within his arms. "Please, Karly don't cry. I promise to take care of you. You've got nothing to worry about, from here on out… *darling.*"

CHAPTER 9

Darling, It's You!

Darling…

Darling…

Darling…

Jake said the magic word. *Darling*. It was *him*! Jake was the one watching over me at the hospital during my coma. He was the one monitoring me. Always protecting me. Constantly checking on me. Even at the party, he was the one who caught me. The one who warned me. It was him. It was *always him*.

"It's *you*," I cry, as I look up at him. "*Darling… it's you!*"

And then, suddenly, *everything* comes back to me in full scale. I can remember it *all* now, most clearly. No longer are the past three years a mysterious and blackened blur. Instead, I remember it. The good, the bad and the ugly.

I remember my unhappy marriage to Brent. The affairs, the lies and the scandals. I recall the divorce proceeding and my estranged husband's approval of it. But more than anything, I also remember Jake and…

I really did love him! And he loved me, too! I remember him being that special person, who helped me to pick up the broken pieces to my failing marriage. He was the one who always lent me his shoulder to cry on. The one who fed me chicken soup, when I was ill. Or the person who brought me tea in the middle of the night. The person who stood by my side, when there was no one left standing. He was my everything and I was his. We were, and still are, soul mates.

And to top it all off, we were supposed to marry, too! I was planning to divorce Brent. He was going to remarry Abigail and I was to remarry Jake. This marriage was over from the very start. I just couldn't remember!

"Jake, I… I remember…" I say with a beaming smile. "I remember you. Me. Us."

Without another word, his lips come crashing down on to mine. His kiss is so fierce and passionate, too. It's filled with such longing and suppressed desire. It's a kiss that I've written a million times over in my romance novels, but had yet to truly experience it for myself… at least, not until *now*.

And before I know it, I surrender myself over to him. And now, one way or another, my best friend has finally graduated to become my new lover… and the rest… is well… magical…

***

Hours later, I get a text from Abigail asking about my whereabouts. By now, it's midnight and Jake is soundly sleeping in the bedroom. Meanwhile, I'm in the kitchen and drinking a glass of water. Even though I can recall most of my past, there's still one thing that remains a mystery. Who was behind the wheel on that fateful day? Who was it exactly, that's responsible for my accident?

Even though the culprit still hasn't yet been caught; but either way, deep within my heart, I just know that it wasn't a true accident. It was intentional.

Meanwhile, as I sit down at the kitchen table, I try to replay that day over again in my mind. From what I do recall, I went to visit Brent at his office in Capitol Hill. It was about the divorce. By then, I already knew about him and Abigail. He was about to agree to our stipulations and then…

Wait a second… the money… it wasn't *his*! All this time, I foolishly assumed that Brent was wealthy and that my income somehow depended upon his… but no. The money, the mansion, the cars… it was all *mine*. I was the wealthy one, not him!

Suddenly, I gasp. I'm shocked. But then again, I shouldn't be. After all, my novels sold thousands of copies world-wide. My wealth… Brent's wealth… they come from my royalties. I am the heiress, not him!

And now, I remember why Abigail was yelling at me on that fateful day. She was carrying a bouquet of red roses, which were *her* favorite… not mine. She didn't want me to divorce Brent. Because divorcing him, meant his loss of income. No, Abigail wanted to be his mistress, while I remained as his wife or else…

And then, I finally *remember*. It was Abigail behind the wheel. She ran me over. Smilingly. She *intentionally* hit me in the parking lot of Capitol Hill, with the sole intention of *killing me. Murdering me* in cold blood to stop the divorce. To make Brent a wealthy widower.

Suddenly, the doorbell rings. Without thinking, I automatically open it and to my horror, I see Abigail standing before me. Smilingly, she's holding a shiny and silver gun that's pointed right at my direction!

CHAPTER 10

Fucking Die, Already!

"**A**bigail?" I choke.

How stupid was I to blindly open the front door in the middle of the night! Of course, she'd have figured out that I was hiding here with Jake. After all, as Brent's assistant, she knew it all, first-hand.

"Do you finally remember now?" she asks me.

"Yes, I do," I tell her, with my chin held up high. "It was you behind the wheel on that day."

"Yes, it was I," Abigail says proudly, with a beaming smile.

"And now," she continues, "I'm here to finish a job."

Within the blink of an eye, Abigail kicks me in my stomach. Instantly, I crash land down on to the floor, knocking a lamp with me along the way. As the fallen lamp shatters across the foyer, I manage to grab a broken piece.

Meanwhile, Abigail is standing, hovering above my head and waving her gun right at me. She intends to kill me. To finish me off, once and for all…

"Karly Summers," she says, "It's time to meet your maker."

Is this the end? After surviving my last accident, overcoming my coma and finding love again, is this truly how my life is going to end? To be murdered in cold blood, by my husband's lover, of all people?

Death might still be in store for my future, but right now, I won't give Abigail the satisfaction. Because tonight, I simply refuse to die. And certainly, not by the hands of this homewrecker!

"I will not die!" I yell at her.

And then, using all of my force, I leap forward and tackle her back down with me to the floor.

"God damn it, Karly!" Abigail shouts, as she falls flat down on to the ground. Dropping her gun to the floor in the process.

For a few solid seconds, we wrestle. She grabs at my hair, while I throw a few hard punches to her face. For all her worth, Abigail is no fighter. She might be the owner of a gun, but without, she's absolutely powerless. Honestly, it's pathetic.

"Fucking die, already!" she yells at me, as blood drips from her nose.

"Never!" I scream, as I throw another fist punch to her swollen face.

By now, I've got her in a choke hold. And a second later, I see from the corner of my eye, Jake is standing right next to me. And most fortunately, he has now, taken possession of Abigail's weapon.

With the gun directly pointed towards Abigail, he simply says, "It's over Abigail. The police are already on their way. It's time to surrender."

And just like that, I'm smiling ear-to-ear, as I watch my enemy crumble into pieces, just like the broken lamp before me. In the end, Abigail Rose finally surrenders and then, she weeps like a baby.

***

The police have arrived and Abigail Rose is now in handcuffs. At long last, my culprit has been caught and now, I can finally sigh a breath of relief. It's all over. Case closed.

Even with the sounds of sirens surrounding us, I turn to Jake's side and place a tender kiss alongside his lips. And while the world around us might be swirling in scandal, with the reporters scribbling down notes for their latest headlines or the police officers writing up their reports, none of it matters. For once, I'm lost in the moment and in the end, I realize that the life of being a senator's wife isn't for me. It's never been.

But instead, perhaps, being the wife of a quiet and low-key accounting attorney is. And for that, I'm willing to give it a try.

CHAPTER 11

Happily Ever After

Two Months Later

Jake and I have since married and as of now, we are touring the English countryside for our honeymoon. In honor of my romance novels, Jake decided to humor me by personally escorting me to visit Jane Austen's former home in Bath. If ever there was a real-life Mr. Darcy, then Jake is mine.

After Abigail's arrest, Brent and I went forward with our divorce. And thanks to Jake's good friend, attorney Blake Everett, our divorce was filed and quickly settled, all within the span of a single month. Imagine that!

Although Brent might not have been the most faithful of husbands, but to his credit, he was completely ignorant about Abigail's crimes. My ex might not be the cleverest of men, but he's no criminal. In the end, he still has a good heart. Not only did he give me his blessing to marry Jake (not that I ever needed his blessing to begin with; but still, it was nice to have it, either way. Especially, on account of him being Jake's former stepbrother and all), but he also didn't ask me for any alimony payments, either. Thankfully. Instead, Brent found himself another new wealthy partner. An expat royal from overseas.

As for me, I'm now happily married to the right man and working on finishing my latest novel. And in case you're wondering, yes, my characters, Jacob, the Duke of Cornwall, and Karoline, the Countess of Mulberry, do get a happily ever after, after all. A happily ever after, just like Jake and I got.

And lastly, each night, when I finally close my eyes to sleep next to my new husband, I find great comfort in the fact that once I wake up the next morning, it will be him by my side and no one else. My own *darling* husband. And honestly, I wouldn't have it any other way.

The End.

Sneak Preview #1

Cupid's Serenade

CHAPTER 1

Once upon a time, there was a fair maiden named Kordelia Silverheart, who had long silvery hair, violet eyes, pale skin and lived at Mount Olympus. Like all of the children of Aphrodite and Ares, Kordelia was a cupid. Along with her many siblings, including her famous brother, Eros, and her most beloved sister, Melissa, Kordelia was tasked with the important duty to serve as a champion matchmaker and a defender of true love, just like the rest of her ancestors before her.

While mythology might not have been so familiar with her own particular name, Kordelia was surprisingly the true matchmaker behind some of the world's most legendary couples, famously known throughout the ages. From Cleopatra and Marc Antony to Arthur and Guinevere, Robin Hood and Maid Marian to Romeo and Juliet, Henry VIII and Anne Boleyn to Shah Jahan and Mumtaz, and Sultan Suleiman and Hurrem— she was single-handily responsible for all of these memorable love pairings.

Ah, yes, Kordelia was a superior cupid. An absolute legend in her own right. Her talents for matchmaking were a true art. It was a subject that she greatly excelled in, and her superior talents proved unparallel.

As a faithful champion and defender of true love, Kordelia believed wholeheartedly in the power and magic of it. The relentless ability for love to transform all individuals into becoming a better version of themselves. For the lonely souls to be reunited with their better halves. Or for the villainous foes to be redeemed through the act of unconditional love. True love was always the solution.

Yes, according to Kordelia, *love* was the *cure for all*. A medicine to the broken hearted. A final wish upon a shooting star. A dream gifted to all, regardless of one's age, class, creed, religion or nation. Love was the key to all of life's mysterious pursuits; for without it, humanity itself, would cease to exist.

Having been born as one of the many daughters of Aphrodite and Ares, Kordelia grew up surrounded by love, in all of its various forms. While history might only remember her parents' famous names, along with her famed brother, Eros; her legendary parents had actually, in fact, bore many, many other children. Over a million and counting… but unfortunately, due to a cupid's secretive nature, most mortals remained completely ignorant about their very existence.

But this wasn't so incredibly surprising. After all, cupids, like Kordelia, were advised by their parents to remain perfectly anonymous and to stay silently hidden from behind the shadows, whenever they were on active duty. It was bad enough that their own grandfather, Zeus, possessed a notorious and flamboyant reputation as a devious rake. Especially, amongst the female mortals.

Therefore, as a result of their grandfather's rogue behavior, Aphrodite and Ares advised their children to refrain from such frivolous and scandalous actions— at least, if they could help it. As professional cupids, their expected duties were to simply blend in amongst the crowd, do their magic and then, gracefully move on.

As immortals, Kordelia and her cupid siblings were all born with extraordinary talents. Like the other gods and goddesses at Mount Olympus, all cupids possessed the same supernatural abilities like the rest of their fellow Olympians. However, in Kordelia's case, she, along with her siblings, primarily used their magical gifts for the sole purposes of matchmaking.

In fact, they seldom ever used their magic selfishly for themselves— although, had they wanted to, then they most certainly could. Eventually, once their assigned mortal was matched to another mate, then their role as their guardian cupid was over and done. Shortly afterwards, they were expected to quickly move on to the next person on their never-ending list, concerning the game of love. Ah, the politics of love…

Over the past several centuries, Kordelia matched well over a million couples and counting, throughout her many visits down to earth. While some of her matched couples became world famous— memorialized in various fairy tales, romantic novels and history books— others remained anonymous, choosing to live their lives more quietly, as normal couples. Furthermore, while love was an *art* that Kordelia had all but perfected; somehow, love nowadays was becoming much more difficult to achieve.

Amazingly enough, love in the past was far easier to match, for people back then, were far simpler to please. In Roman times, a casual batting of the eyelash by a female was enough to draw the wanted attention of a battling gladiator. Even in the medieval era, the love shared between a lady and a knight was so simple and pure; for a single drop of their handkerchief onto the floor was sufficient enough to unite a knight with his new lady lover. Furthermore, Regency and Victorian London was far less complicated, too. In fact, a lovely bouquet of fresh flowers, along with a handwritten love letter, as gifted by a gentleman was plenty enough to claim the heart of a young debutante.

Ah yes, love in the past was far easier than today's current distressful state. In the past, cupids used to frequently travel down to earth with their bows and arrows in hand and within seconds, they were able to match their new couples together within the blink of an eye. But alas, a lot has changed since then.

Nowadays, all cupids have since abandoned their bows and arrows, in exchange for their magical cloud of smoke, known simply as the *cupid's kiss.* Apart from traveling down to earth with less bulky equipment, a cupid's kiss is what immortals like to refer to as their advanced method of matchmaking.

While mortals have since transitioned from writing letters on traditional paper over to emails using computers, cupids have also equally traded in their bows and arrows for their special kiss. A cupid's unique thumbprint, for say. Ultimately, upon securing their love matches, each cupid is gifted with their rare ability to exercise their own special cupid's kiss onto their chosen humans.

With the simple release of their breath through their lips, a pink misty cloud in the shape of a heart is discharged out into the air. Afterwards, it slowly travels down to the direction of both the assigned mortal and their new mate. Once the cupid's kiss takes hold on the new couple, a love match is made. Afterwards, the responsible cupid is expected to return back home to Mount Olympus and wait for their next assignment at the Fountain of Destiny.

Sounds simple and straight forward, right? Well, not so much. As stated before, love in the past was far easier to achieve, for humans back then were much simpler to please. Nowadays, in the twenty-first century, humans, most unfortunately, lack belief. A key ingredient to the magic of true love.

With the distraction of life's daily pursuits, most mortals have practically forsaken the very grand spirit of true love. As a result, their lack of belief has made it far more difficult for cupids to do their jobs effectively. In the end, if people lose their faith in love and ultimately, come to reject it, then how can cupids, like Kordelia, ever successfully come to convince them otherwise?

Furthermore, mortals today no longer even believe in the magic of their legendary cupids anymore. In fact, today's mortals hardly celebrate Valentine's Day, in the first place. In the past, this romantic holiday was once regarded as both a human's and a cupid's favorite day of the entire calendar year. It was a day, in which humans used to call upon on their guardian cupids for assistance to help write romantic love letters, draft heartfelt poetry, arrange an enchanting floral bouquet and work to woo their darling mates into a marriage proposal. Once upon a time, Valentine's Day was equally beloved by cupids too, for each love match that was made on this special day, a new infant cupid was born at Mount Olympus, simultaneously.

Sadly, those days are now long over. People aren't as excited about Valentine's Day, as they once were in the past. Unfortunately, because of this, cupids are forced to become more creative. To think and do outside of the traditional box, for say. For example, before when life was simpler, it was easy to make a love match; for a farmer's son could easily be paired with the neighboring farmer's daughter. But now, cupids must search far and wide, using all of their available resources to secure a proper love match.

However, in twenty-first century earth, people are generally more spread-out, isolated and addicted to their technologies. Unfortunately, as a result, this has made it all the more challenging for cupids to execute their love matches with ease. After all, if humans aren't willing to freely tear their eyes away from their screens, even for a split second, then how can they dare take notice of a new potential love match standing right in front of them, when presented with the opportunity?

While most mortals might have forgotten about the art of love; cupids, on the other hand, have not. As cupids, it is their duty to remain as the champions and defenders of true love, regardless of the dire circumstances. If mortals fail to recognize love nowadays, that only means that they must work harder behind the scenes to secure their love matches. Even if it takes them longer to do it.

Years ago, a typical love match might have taken a cupid only a single afternoon to achieve. However, nowadays, it may take up to a week and in some rare cases, even a whole month! But regardless, cupids not only still believe in true love, many of them have also discovered love for themselves, too. In fact, most cupids already have a mate of their very own... all except for our heroine, Kordelia.

Although many cupids married their fellow Olympians; Kordelia, the princess and champion of love, with her mother, Aphrodite, reigning as queen, ironically, never did. Even though Kordelia was the author to many heartwarming romantic fairy tales and epic love stories; she, herself, was a stranger to it. In reality, Kordelia never experienced true love, let alone, any real sort of romantic adventure, firsthand.

It wasn't that love was forbidden to her, because it wasn't. Truthfully, she just never had the time for it. She was always busy. Even as a cupid, Kordelia took her role very seriously. Often, she was usually too busy to take the careful time to notice any potential partners within her vicinity. Although, to be fair, over the years, she did have a few notable admirers, including the mighty Hercules. But, unfortunately, all of them failed to move her attention. And most importantly, none of them ever managed to capture *her heart*.

Strangely enough, for the woman who was the best at finding love for others, she couldn't even find it for herself. But that was perfectly alright. Truthfully, Kordelia was happily content with her single status. In fact, by her not being so directly attached to love, Kordelia considered herself to be a better matchmaker for it. After all, without the distraction of love, she believed her single status made her a force to be reckoned with, because it allowed her to be more focused and determined to succeed.

While cupids don't generally keep score with their love match success rates; however, for every eight out of ten couples that Kordelia matched, those fortunate couples usually remained a happy pair for the rest of their earthly lives. Meanwhile, the other two remaining couples either died an early tragic death, or were forever romanticized in history as a once beloved and world-famous duo— such as the case with Henry VIII and his second wife, Anne Boleyn.

Surprisingly, one of those couples was her own brother, Eros, and his wife, Psyche. It was actually Kordelia, who was responsible for their chance encounter behind the scenes, all those many years ago. While mythology might credit her brother, Eros, as the hero who relentlessly pursued Psyche, as a personal request of their envious mother, that wasn't entirely the true case. According to legend, Aphrodite was supposedly jealous over Psyche's timeless beauty and therefore, ordered her son to kill the young maiden. However, the actual truth to this popular tale is vastly different and the real story is far less sinister.

The real story, something that's hidden away from popular culture and famed mythology, is that Psyche was, in fact, actually *one* of Kordelia's many *assigned mortals*. In truth, it was Kordelia's responsibility, as her guardian cupid, to match Psyche with a love mate. Naturally, Psyche, being a mortal princess and the daughter of a late king, Kordelia was inclined to pair her with another famous prince from a neighboring kingdom.

However, by the time Kordelia reached into her sack to retrieve an arrow for her bow (back then, in Hellenic Ancient Greece, cupids still used their bows and arrows on active duty; an era that predates the modern cupid's kiss), to her surprise, she saw her brother, Eros. Silently, she watched as her elder brother interacted with a young Psyche down by the river.

Although Eros wasn't expected to accompany her down to earth; somehow, he got news from their sister, Melissa, that Kordelia was set to match one of earth's most beautiful woman with a new mate. Curious as to who this enchanting mortal woman was, out of his own free will and selfish desire, Eros transformed into his humanly form and descended down to earth.

For those, who aren't aware, a cupid taking on their humanly form isn't so much of a physical change. Apart from abandoning their heavenly golden aura at the foot of Mount Olympus, there isn't much else required for a transformation. Unlike popular belief, cupids, like the rest of their fellow Olympians, do *not* have wings. Again, for clarity, I repeat, cupids do *not* have wings. Now that we've cleared that up, shall we, dear reader, continue on?

And so, with much determination, Eros arrived down onto earth. Before Kordelia came to the scene, he quickly made his moves to seek and converse with Psyche. And just as if fate, herself, had played a sly hand at their chance encounter, it was there by the Haliacmon river, where the couple met each other for the very first time… and truly, it was love at first sight…

Initially, Kordelia was greatly annoyed by her brother's meddling interference with her affairs. However, as she silently observed them from afar, Kordelia couldn't help but notice a spark naturally ignite between them. Even though they were two perfect strangers from opposite worlds, they were still organically drawn to each other. Attracted to one another, just like magnets.

Without the use of her bow and arrow, Eros and Psyche magically captured one another's attentions, without the intervention of a cupid… or anything else for that matter. Surprisingly, they were simply enchanted by one another, as evident by their joyful facial expressions. As Kordelia silently watched on, she saw a bright light shine within their eyes, while their smiles stretched from ear-to-ear. Overall, they simply glowed, like a burning star bursting out in the night sky.

Alas, it was there, at that precise moment, when Kordelia came to realize that perhaps, in some unique and rare cases, love was something that was completely spontaneous and natural. It didn't require an intervention by a cupid. It didn't require assistance from anyone else, either. *Love* was *simple*. It was *effortless*. It was *true*.

However, rather than doing nothing, Kordelia couldn't risk

waiting for another male mortal to come and claim Psyche as his own bride. And so, for once, Kordelia had a change of heart and out of compassion, she took pity on her brother. Against her own better judgment, she decided to help him. To secure a love match between himself and the mortal princess, Psyche.

Without another thought, Kordelia decided to take swift action. Instantly, she aimed straight ahead and then, she released an arrow from her bow. In one powerful and magical aim, Kordelia managed to strike both Eros and Psyche right through their hearts simultaneously, with one use of a single arrow.

And at this point in the story, one might presume that the rest is history… but that would be a complete *lie*. For the rest of this story is far more *complicated*, than just an easily achieved happily ever after…

After sealing their fates together, unbeknownst to Kordelia, her bold decision to match an immortal god with a mortal woman proved to be a *real challenge*. A first of their kind. As the favorite son of Aphrodite and Ares, Eros could not forfeit his world, in exchange for a mortal life in Psyche's earthly realm.

Furthermore, the same sacrifice also proved challenging for Psyche, as well. As the daughter of a great king, it was also equally difficult for her to abandon her family and kingdom behind to join Eros at Mount Olympus. However, as difficult as this choice was; in the end, that's precisely what Psyche did: she left her world for his.

Unfortunately, leaving earth for Mount Olympus isn't so simple— especially, for mortals. The secret to Mount Olympus is that mortals aren't designed to co-exist in their heavenly realm; let alone, permitted to freely enter into it. At least, not in their humanly forms.

Following her heart, Psyche ultimately decided to abandon her mortal realm to join the immortal world of her husband's. But, to do so, Psyche was required to drink a special elixir, derived from the Fountain of Destiny. The *elixir to eternal life*. A drink that ultimately, transformed her mortal self into an immortal goddess.

However, dear reader, it's important to note, that once this decision is made, it can never be undone. Once you've chosen to become another immortal out of your own free will, then there can be no reversal… no going back…

And so, as Eros' younger sister, Kordelia, offered Psyche the rare opportunity to drink the elixir to eternal life; she, in return, happily accepted it. Although one might assume that the end result was a grand happily ever after… but… no… that wasn't exactly the case. No, there's still more to this story…

After drinking the elixir to eternal life, Psyche transformed into an immortal cupid god, just like her husband before her. After reuniting with Eros at Mount Olympus, Psyche slowly transitioned into her new role as a fellow cupid. Although she tried her best to adapt into Eros' immortal realm— a world, in which he was conveniently born into; whereas, she clearly wasn't— needless to say, she struggled. While she tentatively listened and actively studied her new profession most eagerly with her fellow cupids; but sadly, behind her smiling face, she secretly grappled to adapt into her new world.

Although Psyche was madly in love with her husband; however, at the same time, she also grew incredibly homesick. Eventually, in time, she came to long for a reunion with her mortal family. Unfortunately, in the bitter end, Psyche came to miss her old world and the life that she previously left behind.

But apart from all of this, Psyche also struggled to fit into her husband's godly family. A family, culture and tradition that was still so incredibly foreign to her. Even though Eros' parents and siblings accepted her without any complaints; however, at the end of the day, she was still a foreigner to them. A stranger. After all, she wasn't a natural born cupid. Instead, she was a convert, turned into a cupid— all due to her undying love and devotion to their brother and son.

Witnessing the sadness stemming from his wife's endless tears, Eros swore to take swift action. He was determined to help alleviate Psyche's ongoing pain and suffering. And so, he did… and *this,* dear reader, are why *legends are born. This* is the *real reason* as to why the Eros and Psyche love story became so epic and famous… it's because of his serenade. The *cupid's serenade.*

While their tale on earth might greatly differ in its retelling over the years, the real reason as to why their love was so grand and memorable, especially at Mount Olympus, was all because of Eros' serenade to Psyche. His *cupid's serenade.*

To better comprehend the significance to the serenade, one must first understand the basic stages to the *art of romance*— particularly, the *ten stages to love*: the chance encounter; curiosity; desire; attraction; lust; yearning; devotion; madness; partnership and last but certainly, not in the least, the serenade.

Starting with the *chance encounter,* this is the first stage when the two lovers initially come to meet. Two perfect strangers, who previously had zero intentions of ever crossing paths with one another, are ultimately forced to do so, all because of fate's direct intervention. At this stage, the couple will experience a spontaneous spark that quickly transforms into a fluttering butterfly feeling, that brews deep within the pits of their nervous stomachs.

Soon afterwards, the *curiosity* phase kicks in. At this stage, the couple will start to innocently wonder about the other person. They'll want to know everything about their prospective partner. And once they discover about their past histories, preferences, hobbies and lifestyles, a friendship between the two are formed.

As their curiosities intensifies, it quickly transforms into the *desire* stage. At this point, the couple develops an overwhelming desire to uncover every last bit of information about their lover. Including but not limited to, their deepest secrets and darkest fears.

Afterwards, the *attraction* phase ignites. After growing accustomed to their new mate, a lover will start to feel a physical gravitation pull towards them. From there, a person will develop an attraction to them.

Moving onwards, after attraction comes *lust*. At this stage, physical passion takes center attention. From this phase onwards, couples will graduate onto a fulltime lover's status and thus, a real physical romantic relationship takes flight. Their relationship as a real couple is recognized and celebrated by both parties.

At this point, love can diverge onto two separate pathways: breakup or commitment. Couples will either find their romance start to fizzle down and will choose to breakup, or they will decide to stay together and sail away through the storm. Ultimately, for the ones who successfully stay together, then this is where true love takes form.

From here on out, love consumes the heart in its entirety. As a result, the heart begins to *yearn* for their partner. During this stage, devoted couples will constantly seek to be next to one another. And whenever they're apart, they'll desperately long for each other, until they're finally reunited.

After experiencing the yearning sensation, we enter into the *devotion* stage. At this phase, the lovers become completely dedicated to their committed relationship. As a result, they will grow ignorant to their partner's faults. Good or bad. As far as they're concerned, in their eyes, their partner will be completely flawless and absolutely perfect, just as they are. Regardless, as to how true or false the reality might be.

Eventually, this extreme emotion will slowly transition into the *madness* stage, in which the lovers won't be able to envision a life beyond each other's shadows. As a result, there will be an overwhelming urge to remain by each other's constant side at all times.

Soon enough, madness transitions into the *partnership* stage. From here on out, the couple will no longer view themselves as individuals, but as two halves to a single coin. At this stage, most formal marriage proposals are made.

Lastly, but most importantly, is the final stage: the public proclamation of true love. A sonnet written by the king of kings themselves: the *serenade.*

Now, dear reader, you've probably already heard of *a* serenade before. For example, Romeo playing a fine tune outside of Juliet's balcony, in an effort to woo his desired lady's heart. Or a hopeful and starry-eyed youth playing a violin for his beloved girlfriend on Valentine's Day. No, this version of the serenade is something else entirely. Because, dear reader, in the game of love, the serenade holds a very special and sentimental meaning. Especially, for us, cupids.

According to cupids, the *serenade* is the *ultimate and final* public declaration of true love. An announcement that one's chosen partner is their soul mate. A proclamation of love, that once uttered out loud, it can never be undone. It's permanent. It's finite. It's proudly announced to all members of society and is celebrated for it. Memorialized in the history books and romanticized in classical fairy tales.

Truthfully, not everyone achieves this special and honorable status. Not all love stories, even the most epic of tales, reaches this final destination. It's achieved only by a few selective and blessed souls.

But let's return back to Eros and Psyche, shall we? As you may recall, Psyche previously abandoned her mortal world, in exchange for Eros' eternal realm. However, by doing so, as a direct consequence of her actions, Psyche struggled to adapt. While the cupids were generally tolerable of her— apart from Kordelia and Melissa, who were both considered to be her dearest of friends— the rest were *not* as welcoming.

Feeling homesick and lacking a warm community, Psyche gradually fell into depression. Sadly, she secretly came to long for her old mortal life back on earth. Although she loved her husband dearly, she still struggled to fit in. Sensing his wife's internal pain and despair, Eros took upon himself to remedy the situation.

After carefully listening to his advisors found throughout their great land, Eros devised a plan. One day, he summoned all of the cupids, including his parents, Aphrodite and Ares, to a festival that he decided to hold. This extravagant festival, a first of its kind, was held near the Fountain of Destiny. And upon their arrival to this milestone event, everyone was left speechless and stunned by the spectacular sight before them.

Much to their astonishment, the venue was decorated with garlands of crimson red roses, dark blue violets, bright yellow marigolds, soft white daisies and sugar pink carnations. In addition, there were also bold red ribbons, shimmering silver lace tablecloths and sparkling gold candles, opal white crystals and other various celebrative objects on display. Never before in their collective history, had Mount Olympus held such a lavishing and exquisite banquet to date. Truly, this was a party fit for the gods!

While Mount Olympus might have been the home to the various gods and goddesses of mythology, such parties and décor were seldom used within their own land. Instead, they were primarily reserved for their endless missions and voyages down on earth. However, on that memorable day, this wasn't the case. For once, Mount Olympus was showered with the most luxurious goods that were often reserved for the most enchanting of fairy tales.

Once everyone arrived to the venue, Eros commanded the orchestra to play the sweetest of melodies, using their harps, violins and piano instruments. And as they played their romantic tunes, Eros removed a red velvet cloak to reveal a floral golden throne, featured in the center of the banquet. This golden throne was adorned with crimson red roses encircling it all around, forming one large gigantic garland. Truly, it was a throne fit for a queen.

As Psyche graciously took her seat, Eros publicly declared his eternal love and devotion to her. In his speech, Eros thanked Psyche for her relentless loyalty and dedication to their marriage, as well as her personal sacrifice to forfeit her world to join his side at Mount Olympus. In return, he vowed to remain loyal and faithful to her, forever more.

Lastly, but most importantly, Eros reverted his attention over to the audience. From the bottom of his heart, he pleaded with them to accept Psyche not only as his wife, but as a fellow cupid— one of their equals. In exchange, Eros vowed to remain as their loyal and faithful brother. Furthermore, if they promised to welcome his new wife into their hearts, then he'd be forever grateful to them.

Touched by his sincere proclamation to both his wife and family, everyone at the banquet, including their parents, graciously accepted his generous offer. From that day forward, things vastly improved for Psyche. Everyone tried harder to welcome her into their community and many cupids sought to even forge a real friendship with her. In the end, everyone who lived at Mount Olympus were a lot kinder and more appreciative of her.

And this, dear reader, was the very first and only cupid's serenade in all of history. A proclamation made by Eros to his beloved wife, Psyche. A public declaration of their marital union, between the body and the soul. The mind and the heart. Ultimately, this was the special day that marked the beginning to their grand and epic love story, making the famous pair: Eros and Psyche.

While Mount Olympus might recall this event as the *first cupid's serenade* in our history books; however, by the time this tale eventually reached the ears of men down on earth, the story vastly changed, with several key milestone facts altered. As a result, various iterations and alternative endings to the beloved Eros and Psyche tale were shared and told under new and often times, conflicting narratives. Sadly, many of the key important highlights were either purposely excluded from the retelling, or completely lost in translation.

Over the centuries, due to the numerous cupids traveling back and forth between Mount Olympus and earth, each cupid shared with the humans a different rendition to the famous serenade. Eventually, once these alternative versions grew more widespread in the land of men, the story itself, changed and evolved so much that over time, the original tale, as written down onto paper, is almost unrecognizable by those who were actually there in-attendance on that milestone day and bore witness to this ceremonial event.

Therefore, the version of Eros and Psyche known in today's Greek mythology on earth is vastly different, than the actual true version that took place thousands of years ago at Mount Olympus. And, our heroine, Kordelia Silverheart, will be the first to attest to this, too.

Lastly, you might be curiously wondering, as to which methodologies do cupids typically choose to exercise, when pairing a soul to another being? Well, the short answer is that they can either research their assigned human ahead of time at the Library of Souls, or they can simply wait for their arrival down onto earth. From there, they can watch and observe their humans from behind their shadows and later on, make a final decision on whom to match their assigned mortal with.

To reach that final decision regarding a proper mate, each cupid will silently study their mortal, paying close attention to their unique mannerisms and personalities, as well as their likes and dislikes. From there, a cupid is generally able to successfully make a love match, similar to how a doctor studies their patient and then, after diagnosing them with a specific ailment, they proceed to prescribe them with a remedy. After all, what else could be the greatest of cures other than true love, above all else?

But gradually, over this past century, Kordelia was starting to find the art of love to be a bit more challenging than ever before. Although assigning love might appear easy to most outsiders; but guaranteeing that a love match will endure the test of time and last forever is truly a gamble.

However, this never stopped Kordelia, a champion and defender of true love; for she knew, that someone, somewhere out there, was a soul mate just waiting to be united with another person. A silent wish upon the stars for a chance to unite with their one true love.

In the meantime, as Kordelia sat near the Fountain of Destiny to wait for her next assignment, she couldn't help but remember about Eros' and Psyches' epic love story. Was it truly possible for true love to withstand the test of time, just like her brother and sister-in-law had done so successfully?

After all, most mortals only lived for a limited amount of time on earth. Therefore, a human's capacity to love was only meant to last for no more than a single lifetime. But, in a cupid's case, love was eternal; for they were immortals. Love never ended for them; for they never died.

However, today, at this very moment, Kordelia began to ponder as to whether or not a mortal could actually fall in love with another being for more than a single lifetime. Was it possible for a human to love someone, for all eternity? Was such a thing even remotely possible? Especially, for humans in modern times? In a land, where love struggled to take hold? In a world, where belief was scarce? And happily ever afters rare?

Furthermore, Kordelia also wondered that had her fellow cupids chosen not to interfere with humans, then was it still possible for mortals to naturally fall in love with one another, without the use of their magic? And if cupids weren't responsible for assigning love to mortals, then what exactly constituted true love to begin with?

Meanwhile, Kordelia eagerly stared away at the floating waters above the Fountain of Destiny, as she waited for her next assignment's name to appear. As it would just so happen, this was the normal routine for all cupids. To silently and ever-so patiently sit at the Fountain of

Destiny and wait. Wait… and… wait… and wait…

And so, as Kordelia continued to patiently wait and watch, she curiously wondered who her next assignment was going to be. Would he be pretty or ugly? Kind or mean? Rich or poor? Young or old? Honestly, Kordelia simply couldn't help but remain ever-so-curious.

Finally, after much prolonged waiting, a name appeared. Written in all gold letterings, her chosen mortal's identity appeared at long last. His name was Dr. Peter Murphy— Kordelia's next assignment.

"What are you doing?" asked Melissa, her sister, as she joined Kordelia by the side of the fountain.

"I was waiting for my next assignment," replied Kordelia. "And it looks like I just got it."

Leaning down against the fountain, Melissa took a peek at the name and to Kordelia's astonishment, her sister's eyes actually widened and then, she gasped.

"Is something wrong?" asked Kordelia, concerned by her sister's unpleasant reaction.

"Is *that* your next assignment?" asked Melissa, in return, with a surprised expression.

"Yes, as a matter-of-fact it is. Why do you ask?" replied Kordelia, now wondering why her sister was acting so strange, upon seeing Peter's name.

"Dr. Peter Murphy," Melissa repeated, "Kordelia are you sure that you want to go through with this assignment? Maybe, you should forgo this one and just wait for another name."

"I can't do that. Besides, I've never done that before. I've always followed the names in the exact order, given to me by the fountain. Why should I alter my regular routine? Especially, now, of all times?"

asked an astonished Kordelia, who was by now, completely perplexed by her sister's blunt opposition to her next assigned human.

"Well... Kordelia, I'm not sure how to break this one to you lightly," Melissa began, as she took in a deep breath. "But my dear sister, since you asked..."

Gazing at her younger sister Melissa, who looked almost identical to her, with the same silvery hair, violet eyes and pale complexion, Kordelia couldn't help but wonder as to why her sister was so troubled by this new assignment of hers. Just what was so wrong about Dr. Peter Murphy, anyways?

"Go on, go ahead and tell me," Kordelia spoke gently, in an effort to help encourage her sister to tell her the truth.

"Well... Peter is a difficult guy... in fact, many cupids have already tried to match him with other mortals, but they all failed each and every time," Melissa revealed.

"Wait, so this isn't the first time that his name has appeared in the Fountain of Destiny?" asked Kordelia, in surprise.

"No, it certainly isn't," laughed Melissa out loud.

And then, she added, "Nor, do I think it'll be his last time, either."

"Melissa, whatever do you mean?" asked Kordelia, now, most intrigued.

"It's just that a hundred other cupids have all tried to match him, but each and every time they tried, they've all miserably failed," sighed Melissa.

"A hundred other cupids? Why haven't I heard about this before?" asked Kordelia, eager to learn more about this new mysterious mortal of hers.

"Because everyone else is ashamed to admit that they've actually failed with him. He's quite difficult, just so you know."

"I see," reflected Kordelia. "But how do you know about all of this? Were you one of them?"

"Me?" asked a surprised Melissa.

"No, not at all," she revealed. "I only just overheard a few of them complain about him. Although his name did appear once for me in the fountain a while back. However, unlike the other cupids, I actually chose to skip over him."

"Skip over his name? Can you even do that? Aren't we all supposed to be the champions of love?"

"Speak for yourself, Kordelia. Not all of us wants a *headache*. And that *man*, my dear sister, is a *headache*," Melissa admitted.

"Dr. Peter Murphy, a headache? Come now, Melissa, you mustn't really mean that!" exclaimed Kordelia.

"Oh, but I do, dear sister. Unlike you, I'm perfectly willing to bow down and back away from a troubled soul," Melissa boldly proclaimed with much conviction, as she folded her arms across her chest.

"The world is already hard enough for us cupids, so why should I bother and set myself up for a sinking ship? Besides, Peter is a hopeless cause. You might as well throw in the towel and wait for another assignment, because that guy is *never* going to fall in love. Not now, not ever."

"Melissa, I simply refuse to give into such a negative outlook!" Kordelia shouted, with passion. "After all, we're cupids! We're the champions of true love! I've never, ever turned my back against a mortal! And I refuse to start now!"

"Suit yourself, my dear sister," spoke Melissa.

"But Kordelia, are you sure that you want to go through with this?" she asked. "You've never failed on a mission before. However, this time around, I'm afraid you might be actually setting yourself up for an epic failure."

"Melissa, if the Fountain of Destiny chose his name for me, then I've got to do it. There's a reason as to why I was chosen to be his cupid. It's fate. I must be his destiny," Kordelia concluded.

"But then, how do you explain all of the other cupids, who have already tried and failed with him, along the way?" asked Melissa, most curiously.

"I can't speak for them," replied Kordelia. "But I can, however, speak for myself. I, Kordelia Silverheart, have never turned a blind eye to true love. Never have and I certainly, won't start now, either. Besides, love has always been a bit of a challenge for the rebellious ones. However, that never stopped me in the past. It never prevented me from pairing the likes of Robin Hood and Maid Marian before, now did it?"

"No, I suppose it didn't," Melissa recalled.

"Either way, perhaps this Peter fellow needs a professional to help him, such as myself. Anyways, it's still worth a try," said Kordelia, with a smile.

"But if you fail, then you won't mind? What about your perfect streak?" asked Melissa, with a concerned expression across her face.

"Melissa, I've never had a perfect streak. But still, I've got to at least try. Besides, who knows, maybe this mission will be my best yet," remarked Kordelia, happily.

"For your sake Kordelia, I really hope you're right," Melissa reflected, as she remained the skeptical sister still left standing out of the two.

And with that, Kordelia bid her sister adieu and prepared for her departure back down to earth. While love matches might have become more difficult over the recent years, Kordelia absolutely refused to turn down a challenge. Not today, not tomorrow… not ever…

After all, as the champion and defender of true love, romance was Kordelia's profession. It's what she did. She was good at her job. Plus, as a true professional, she knew the *art of love*, at best. Besides, as of lately, Kordelia was in need of a real challenge.

At this point, whether Dr. Peter Murphy was interested in love or not, it really didn't matter; for if Kordelia was on the case, then ultimately, even the most skeptical opponents of true love were going to eventually be forced to succumb to it. Truly, this was going to be a battle between the heart and the mind; the body and the soul. Ultimately, this was war and Kordelia, one way or another, was determined to conquer Peter's heart, come hell or high water!

Sneak Preview #2

The Curse of the Dark Horseman

CHAPTER 1

Lady Kassandra Stanton stood firm and still, as she concentrated on the portrait that hung before her. Ever since her childhood, it was a picture that she often admired but yet, knew very little about. Whenever she stood inside the grand salon, located within her family's private estate at Wiltshire Hall, Kassie always sought for a quiet and somber moment to peacefully gaze at the portrait. It was there inside that very room, which was currently owned by her legal guardian and grandmother, Maureen, where the portrait hung. Tucked away in the furthest corner, behind the piano and nearest to the window overlooking the blooming garden attached to her family's grand home, was the precise location as to where Kassie's most beloved and cherished portrait was proudly displayed.

The portrait was that of a dashing young and handsome gentleman on horseback. His hair was as black as night, while his face was as white and as transparent as that of a mere ghost. His eyes were emerald green, just like the hanging ivy vines and sprouting oak tree leaves, which grew in great abundance throughout their remote and sleepy English country village located in Northern England. Additionally, his clothes appeared rather old fashioned and seemed to be at least a hundred years older than the current fashion worn by other similar gentlemen of equal age and social stature as he. Furthermore, seated above his black stallion horse, the 'Dark Horseman'— as Kassie preferred to reference him as — stood right there in the center of the portrait, surrounded by the dark and evergreen forest behind him, along with a blackened and shadowy road in the background and lastly, accompanied by the night sky illuminating right above him.

With the moon shining down upon him as his only source of light, Kassie squinted her eyes and noticed that for the very first time, right there behind the Dark Horseman, situated upon a small hill, appeared to be that of a vast estate. However, due to the dimly painted paint strokes and darkly shadows, it was rather difficult to detect. But there, upon closer inspection, Kassie certainly did see something. Moving her observation away from the estate, Kassie reverted her attention back to the horseman. For some odd reason, she was always pulled to him… like a strange and unexplainable gravitational force that constantly drew her back in and directly towards his path. Whether or not she was interested to look elsewhere in the painting, one way or another, Kassie consistently found herself staring straight at his face— particular at his eyes. For if truth be told, there was something vexing about his eyes that always caught her attention. It was as if, by some odd occurrence, that he was somehow watching her. Impossible, right?

Of course, Kassie, naturally knew better. After all, she was a modern and educated lady, living at the turn of the twentieth century. It was the year 1900. But somehow, by some odd and rare notion, Kassie always felt within her heart that in another lifetime, she knew the Dark Horseman. Really knew him. Personally. More than just as the man, who remained forever frozen in-time on horseback in a simple portrait painted by an unknown artist.

But what was even more strange and peculiar, was that ever since she was a young girl, the Dark Horseman was always in her dreams. Following her. Haunting her. Helping her. Although Kassie seldom hardly ever recalled any of her other dreams; however, whenever it came to the matter concerning the Dark Horseman, she always remembered her dreams about him most vividly well after she awoke, come the next morning.

What were those dreams, pray tell? Well, it was rather difficult to say. Although Kassie vaguely recalled in such little details as to how their original paths crossed; but either way, in each dream, she always found herself on horseback and wandering through the dark and gloomy woods late into the night… lost… alone and… scared. Fearful of the darkness and the mysterious creatures that lurked inside of the woods during the midnight hour, Kassie closed her eyes tightly shut, as she quietly hoped and prayed for a miracle. And then, just before she lost all hope, her prayers were miraculously answered. Furthermore, before Kassie had enough time to even bat an eyelash, the Dark Horseman was off, galloping away from a far-off distance, on his way to rescue her. As soon as he scooped her up within his strong and sturdy arms and then whisked her away with him, Kassie would suddenly awake and return back to her current realm.

Who he was and if he was based on an actual historical figure was something that Kassie always wondered about. Was he rooted upon fiction or was he real? Was he intended to be a good character, or was he designed to be evil? Kassie never really knew the truth to be sure. But either way, whatever the original artist's intentions were, it really didn't matter. For Kassie, the Dark Horseman was good and kind to her. He was her hero, after all. But more than anything, had he been a real man, then Kassie was absolutely certain and convinced that her mysterious horseman would have been her equal match. An ideal husband. That, if he were actually here, standing right before her in real life, then she would have much rather have preferred marrying him than her current fiancé, Walter, in an instant. Walter, a man whom she was engaged to marry, was a union born out of necessity and sadly, not of love. Tragically, this was a harsh reality that many ladies of her time, with similar social and economic backgrounds, had to face: an unwanted engagement due to the pressures of their respected families. But apart from all of this, Kassie remained convinced that had her Dark Horseman been a real man, then her life would have taken a much different course. Furthermore, Kassie also knew within her heart that had her fantasy been an actual reality, then he would have madly loved her and she, in return, would have madly loved him, too.

"Are you still obsessing over that painting?" asked Maureen to her granddaughter, Kassie.

"I thought that I was still alone in the room," Kassie bashfully admitted.

"Ever since you were a young girl, I could never pull you away from that painting," sighed Maureen, as she walked over to join Kassie's side.

"Is he real?" asked Kassie, suddenly and bluntly.

"My dear child," began Maureen, "Whatever do you mean? He's a painting. Of course, he isn't real. He's no more than paint."

"I mean, is he based upon a real person? A historical figure?" Kassie clarified.

"Well, that's more like it," laughed Maureen.

"Well? Is he?" asked Kassie, once more.

"I'm not entirely certain," admitted Maureen. "But personally, I think he might have been."

"Really?" asked Kassie, surprised by her grandmother's admission.

"I've never told you about the legend of the Dark Horseman of Galloway Manor before, now, have I?" asked Maureen, with a raised brow.

"The legend of the Dark Horseman of Galloway Manor…" Kassie excitingly repeated, in amazement.

"From your reaction, I take it that I haven't," said Maureen, as she sarcastically laughed on.

"I suppose," Maureen continued, "That the time has finally come for me to come clean and tell you more about him."

"Wait, so you knew of him?" quickly asked Kassie, in return.

Walking towards her sofa nearby, Maureen decided to take a seat and enjoy a fresh cup of tea; which at this very moment, was conveniently being served right on time for their daily scheduled afternoon tea service.

"Let us discuss more about this matter over some tea," Maureen suggested, as she already began to pour Kassie a cup, without her even agreeing to it.

"One or two lumps of sugar?" asked Maureen, as she placed the teapot back down onto the table.

"None," replied Kassie, with a bold smirk.

"Ah, yes," Maureen laughed on. "That's right. You prefer milk, just like your dear late mother."

"Actually," Kassie interrupted. "It was my late *father's* favorite."

"Yes, I stand corrected. Wise girl," replied Maureen, as she sadly recalled her own son's and daughter-in-law's unfortunate passing.

"Anyways," Maureen continued, "Why don't you come and join me, so that I can share my tale with you."

"Very well," replied Kassie, as she walked over and took a seat nearby her grandmother.

Once Kassie joined her side, Maureen added a dash of milk to her tea and then, she handed her the teacup, along with a small almond biscuit to serve as a side snack. As Kassie took her first sip of her tea, Maureen stared on at the painting, as she prepared to reveal the legend behind the mysterious rider.

"Once upon a time, or so, as they say," she began, "There was a young gentleman, named Lord Henry Galloway of Galloway Manor."

"Wait, so the horseman was based on a real-life person?" Kassie inquired, most curiously.

"Yes, he was," replied Maureen, as she took another sip of her tea.

"Did you know him? In real-life?" asked Kassie, once more.

"Unfortunately, no, as he was around well before my own time," admitted Maureen.

"How long ago?" asked Kassie.

"About a hundred years or so," replied Maureen. "Anyways, it's best that I continue on with the story."

Almost immediately, Kassie nodded her head in agreement. Although Kassie wasn't often considered to be an avid listener; however, this time around, she was all ears. Ah, yes, Kassie was most eager to hear the story of this most intriguing tale.

"A hundred years ago, Galloway Manor was the most lavish, exquisite and famous estate in our entire village; if not, in all of England, for that matter. Naturally, as a result, the Galloway family was one of the wealthiest, respected, famous and most powerful families around. In fact, they owned most of, if not, all the land inside this very village. Amazingly enough, practically everyone living here was once employed by them."

"Really? If so, then why haven't I ever heard of their surname before? Up until now, I've never encountered anyone related to their family. Not once. Let alone, an estate called Galloway Manor," remarked Kassie.

"Well," began Maureen, "A lot can happen over the span of a hundred years."

"What about our family?" Kassie inquired.

"My child, bear a little more patience with me, for I am getting to that," answered Maureen.

"As I was saying," Maureen continued, "A hundred years ago, the Galloways owned everything. The father was an earl, known as the Earl of Galloway, and he had a son named Henry. Lord Galloway was a kind and generous man, who was once married to a distant relative of my mine, named Sarah. Shortly, after Henry's birth, Sarah tragically died from complications associated with childbirth. Naturally, Lord Galloway was devastated by this painful loss, for he loved Sarah unconditionally, with all of his heart. But as unfortunate as this untimely tragedy truly was, Lord Galloway was, at the same time, also blessed with the birth of their only son Henry, who was now the sole heir to his vast ancestral estate, title and fortune. And so, in time, Henry grew up to become a dashingly handsome, educated and well-mannered gentleman. However, for as handsome and as wealthy as Henry was, he was also, just like his father before him, kind and generous to everyone, regardless of their lack of titles or lower social and economic statuses."

"He sounds too good to be true," Kassie reflected.

"Perhaps," added Maureen. "But, like all tales, Henry's upbringing was also filled with several challenges along the way."

"Really? How so?" Kassie inquired, as she remained glued to her grandmother's every passing word.

"Like you, Henry also grew up as an orphan," Maureen revealed. "But before his father's passing, the earl married another woman by the name of Vera. Not much is known about her apart from the fact that she was a foreign-born woman, who was also rumored to have been descended from an ancient Russian family with some traces of gypsy blood in her, too. But from what we do know, during Lord Galloway's many travels to the far east, one day he returned back to our village with a new bride. Through his second marriage to Vera, Lord Galloway sired another son, named Phillip, who was the half-brother to Henry. Naturally, Henry, as the first-born son, remained as the sole heir to his father's title, estate and fortune. However, this did not deter nor minimize, Vera's bitterness and resentful envy of him."

"How unfortunate that must have been," remarked Kassie.

"Yes, how unfortunate that must have been, indeed," agreed Maureen. "Needless to say, unfortunately, Lord Galloway succumbed to an untimely death; a horseback riding accident that left him paralyzed. Sadly, due to his severe injuries, he shortly soon afterwards, fell into a deep coma and never awoke. Many say, that had Vera not been around, then there was a hopeful chance that Lord Galloway might have recovered. But again, these are only speculations."

"Did people honestly believe that there was some sort of foul play?" asked Kassie, most concerned.

"Yes," answered Maureen. "Sadly, that's precisely what the villagers thought. Personally, that's what I believed happened, too. Regardless, upon Lord Galloway's passing, his title, estate and fortune were immediately transferred over to Henry, as his inheritance. However, at the time, Lord Henry was still a young man, who was busy away living abroad and not quite yet ready to manage the daily affairs of Galloway Manor. As a result, his stepmother, Vera, served as the head mistress of the manor, in his absence. Unfortunately, her rule was so cruel and authoritarian, that most of the servants quickly fled the estate soon afterwards. For the ones who reluctantly stayed behind, they were subjected to harsh working and living conditions. Sadly, Vera's cruel nature and heartless administration of the manor went on for several years—up until the arrival of Lord Henry, upon his thirtieth birthday. By this time, Henry was a grown man, who was already well established and ready to take over the rigorous affairs and responsibilities of his late father. However, this didn't sit too well with Vera, who wasn't yet ready to give up her power so easily over to her stepson. A man, who wasn't of her blood, and whom, she regarded, as far less suitable and ideal than her own son, Phillip. Ah, yes, Vera favored Phillip over Henry, and she was most determined to steal Henry's inheritance away and transfer it over to Phillip."

"How dreadfully terrible!" exclaimed Kassie.

"Yes, it was," replied Maureen. "To make matters far worse, Lord Henry was to be engaged. Now, if Henry had married and produced another heir of his very own, then Phillip would have most certainly, stood in no direct chance of ever inheriting Galloway Manor. Therefore, something needed to be done. And so, a curse was enacted."

"A curse?" asked Kassie, in amazement.

"Yes, a curse," confirmed Maureen. "A curse beyond time, space and measure. As for the specific details surrounding the curse, I'm not entirely certain. But from what I do know, Vera was directly responsible for what happened to Lord Henry."

"What happened to him?" asked Kassie.

"On the eve of his wedding, Lord Henry was out riding on horseback through the woods. It was late at night, around the midnight hour. Just like every other night before, dating back from his own childhood, Henry rode his majestic stallion down the open path. However, unlike before, this time around, he failed to return back home."

"What do you mean? Did Henry go missing?" asked Kassie, most intrigued.

"Well," began Maureen, "I suppose this is where the curse begins."

"How so?" asked Kassie, as she took a bite of her almond biscuit.

"As you can safely presume, there was no wedding the following morning; for Henry had long gone missing. Although all of the servants and local villagers searched high and low for Henry, no one could find him," Maureen revealed.

"Did he and his horse run away?" Kassie inquired.

"It's possible, but where could he have gone? Even now, the nearest town isn't for miles on end. Plus, there were no footsteps, nor any horse tracks along the way. One way or another, it seemed like Lord Henry, along with his black stallion, Midnight, simply vanished," said Maureen, as she threw her hands up into the air.

"If Lord Henry vanished, then what became of his family? Why have I never heard of them or their manor, until now?" asked Kassie, while desperately trying to better understand this intriguing tale.

"I'm getting to there, my dear," replied Maureen. "After Henry's disappearance, rumors began to circulate that his fiancé, Julia, and his half-brother, Phillip, were secretly lovers. With Henry out of the picture, Julia and Phillip were free to marry. And so, the couple soon ran off together and eloped to Scotland to marry. Nevertheless, they were never heard of ever again. As for Vera, well… with both Henry and Phillip gone, she remained as the new sole heir and owner of Galloway Manor. But, as my own grandmother use to say, 'evil means will always meet a violent end;' and this holds many truths, especially with regards to Vera. But before I get to Vera, let me first return back to Henry."

"But I thought that Henry was already dead," Kassie interrupted.

"Presumed dead," Maureen corrected.

"Really? How fascinating," Kassie remarked, as she took another sip of her warm tea.

"That night… that fateful night… in which Henry blindly rode out into the forest with his black stallion…was the very night that ultimately came to seal his fate. Although Henry rode a hundred times over before in that same dark and gloomy forest; however, this time around, this was the night, in which Vera finally cornered him… and enacted her curse," Maureen revealed.

"Wait," cried Kassie, in astonishment. "Was Vera a witch?"

"Yes, that she was," replied Maureen, calmly. "She was indeed, a witch. And, a most envious and sinister one, at that."

"How utterly dreadful," Kassie remarked. "What happened to Henry, when he encountered her?"

"Well," Maureen continued, "Just like his father before him, Vera also intended to have Henry killed and then blame his untimely death as an unfortunate 'accident' due to horseback. However, I should also mention, that Vera was a practitioner of black magic; meaning that her powers stemmed from all of the negative energies and dark forces of the earth. In order for Vera to have enacted her powers on that fateful night, she needed to call upon all that was evil, in order to do her bidding. And so, it was there in the middle of the forest, where Vera came face-to-face with Henry. Alas, as she revealed to him her true ugly and witchy form, she also summoned all of the dark powers and energies from the forest to come attack and kill him."

"Fascinating," observed Kassie.

"Yes, it was," agreed Maureen. "Once she committed this evil deed, Vera quickly vanished straight into thin air; all the while, leaving poor Henry and his horse alone to meet their dreadful doom. Meanwhile, as the thick ivy vines, trees and prickly plant thorns sprang up into the air to strangle and squeeze him to death, Lord Henry managed to say a little prayer. Even with the pesky vines suffocating and pressing down against his very throat, Henry still miraculously managed to say his prayer aloud, before his mouth was eventually sealed shut by the protruding leaves that had quickly engulfed him. But Kassie, my dear, please do remember that where there is darkness, there is also light… and where there is evil, there is also good, just waiting right around the corner. Shall I continue on, my child?"

"Yes, please do," Kassie pleaded.

"Very well, as I was saying," Maureen continued, "As the forest continued to consume and devour Henry and his horse, a magical light suddenly appeared. But before Henry could fully comprehend as to what was about to happen next, the forest abruptly ceased attacking him and in no time, all of the vines, plants and trees quickly released their tight hold of him. After Henry was freed from his attackers, he quickly glanced towards the light. To his amazement, he noticed a beautiful woman standing right in front of him. And ironically, this lady also just so happened to resemble his own late mother."

"Wait, was this woman his mother, Sarah?" asked Kassie, in surprise.

"Yes, it was Sarah," Maureen confirmed. "Just like the angel that she was in life, so she was well after her death. Hearing the cries of her son from heaven, Sarah returned back to earth to come to her son's rescue. Although Sarah had freed him from his attackers, she unfortunately couldn't stop the evil and powerful curse that Vera had already enacted. By saving Henry and preventing the forest from consuming him in death, a debt was now owed back to the forest, in exchange: his own mortality. Sadly, with his life having been spared, Henry was now doomed to remain as a creature of the forest; never again permitted to leave its grounds, for all eternity. Was this a fate worse than death? It's hard to say. Needless to say, after his mother revealed this sad but bitter truth to him, Sarah also pleaded with Henry to remain hidden within the forest. In addition, she also forewarned him to never seek revenge on Vera; for if he did, then the consequences of his actions would not only be irreversible, but they would also prove to be regretful. However, Henry, being the determined young man that he was, simply couldn't stand by this injustice and do nothing. And so, after waiting and hiding for one long month inside the forest, Henry eventually returned back to Galloway Manor. Since the estate stood within the same land and forest as his curse, Henry was able to ride home and enter back into his house late into the night. With Vera busy away enjoying her last supper while seated as the new head of the table, Henry abruptly entered the room and without waiting not a second longer, he plunged his dagger straight into her heart, killing her instantly."

"I see, so Henry got his revenge in the end, didn't he?" asked Kassie.

"Yes, he did; but sadly, it also came at a heavy price," Maureen revealed.

"What was the price?" asked Kassie.

"Having acted upon his rash impulses and selfish desire for revenge, Henry most unfortunately and permanently sealed his own fate. By slaying the one woman, who knew the precise remedy to his curse, Henry was now doomed to forever remain bounded to it. Tragically, now, even as I speak, neither sleep nor death, can ever befall upon him. He lives and rides on his horse forever more, as a prisoner of the forest and of Galloway Manor. Time knows no boundaries to him, yet distance does. After that night, most of the servants fled and no one else has seen him or Galloway Manor, ever since. It was as if, both Henry and the manor simply vanished into thin air. That, or, they were all hidden away deep within the forest, where no human eyes can ever lay their sights upon them, ever again."

"If that's the case, then how did this portrait here, come into being?" asked Kassie, with a raised brow.

"Well, long after Vera's death, Galloway Manor, along with its inhabitants were all slowly but surely forgotten. A blemish in history. A forgotten family name and estate. However, the memory of Henry continues to live on, through the legend of the Dark Horseman. In fact, some of our own villagers profess to have actually seen the Dark Horseman occasionally riding out in the forest, so late into the night. Even to this very day, some still claim to have encountered him, face-to-face. For some travelers, they regard him as a saint, coming to help aid them along their night journey through the woods; while for others, he's the very devil, himself, sent to summon them to their violent dooms. But whether he's a saint or the devil, I suppose that's really up to the individual. As for myself, I personally think he's an agent of good. A somewhat gothic and legendary Robin Hood, of sorts."

"I see; so, Lord Henry and his black stallion, Midnight, are the same Dark Horseman and horse from your picture. Furthermore, he's not only a legend, but he's also based on a real person. But still, that doesn't explain as to how you came to acquire this portrait of him?" asked Kassie, who was determined to press on for more concrete answers.

"As I said before," Maureen continued, "His mother, Sarah, was a distant relative of mine. Besides, this portrait was painted well before he became the legendary Dark Horseman."

"Henry seems like an interesting character," Kassie reflected. "I wish that, perhaps, in another lifetime, I could have met him."

"Be careful what you wish for Kassie," Maureen warned. "The curse of the Dark Horseman might be a myth, but magic still runs true in our part of the world. Why, our own village is so incredibly superstitious, that we don't even have any black cats living inside of here! Imagine that!"

"It's because we have more dogs around, used for hunting, that's why," Kassie insisted.

"Perhaps, but the mind is also a powerful force. What you believe, you often see. And what you hope, often comes to be," said Maureen.

"If that's truly the case, then why must I marry Walter?" asked Kassie, with the tone of her voice sounding purely melancholy in nature.

"But don't you care for him?" asked Maureen calmly, in return.

"Walter is kind and decent, but I don't love him. He's just a friend and nothing more," replied Kassie, boldly and as a matter of fact.

"Eventually, in due time, you can grow to love him," Maureen reassured her. "Kassie, I'm not going to live forever and without a mother and a father, I also need to make sure that you're properly taken care of well after I'm gone."

"But I've gone to university. I can take care of myself," Kassie reminded her.

"I have no doubt. However, as a woman, your chances are still limited in your career choice. Plus, our family's estate and fortune will ultimately come to pass over to your male cousin and not you, if we don't take action. Besides, Walter is a family friend and a decent fellow.

He will treat you with respect, which is more than most husbands do," advised Maureen.

"But I don't love him," Kassie cried.

"Love is such a rarity, my dear. Not everyone experiences the same romantic love, as we read in stories. Sometimes, it's far better to live a safe life, than to risk otherwise," Maureen reflected.

"Are you really still insisting that I marry Walter, come tomorrow?" asked Kassie, with desperation in her eyes.

"My dear, you already know my answer. Now, please come to accept it," said Maureen, firmly.

"But…" began Kassie; however, sadly, she couldn't find the words to finish her own thought.

However, her grandmother already knew what was secretly hidden away, within her own heart.

"Kassie," began Maureen, "Men like Henry are legends. They exist only in our romanticized tales. But men like Walter, they're real. My dear girl, please don't waste any more time chasing after your dreams and fairy tale like aspirations, in the hopes of achieving a happy ending. Such endings are not designed for everyone. Kassie, my dear, it's best that you come to accept your reality now, rather than later."

And with that, Maureen got up from the sofa, kissed her granddaughter goodbye and exited out of the salon to retire for the rest of the afternoon. With Maureen gone, Kassie stayed behind and continued to stare and admire the portrait. Just an hour ago, she knew nothing about the Dark Horseman. But now, she practically knew his entire life story. What would it be like to meet a man, who spent the past one hundred years living in a curse? A curse, in which no one knew how to break it? Or that, he was once, a real man? Was he lonesome, or was he content on living his life in solitude? Did he even miss the outside world? Kassie was more curious than ever. Had he not haunted her dreams these past few nights, then Kassie would have reluctantly accepted her fate to marry Walter. But now, as soon as she closed her eyes, she saw only the Dark Horseman, aka Lord Henry Galloway, instead.

Sneak Preview #3

The Ambassador's Wife

CHAPTER 1

On a cold December afternoon, Kate stared outside of her grandmother's window to eagerly watch the snow fall upon her family's garden. Precisely one week ago, their garden was covered in bright sunshine, along with blooming white daisies and tall evergreens that flourished throughout their vast open acres. At that time, the crystal blue sky was adorned with pink and emerald green hummingbirds flying high above in the air, all chirping the sweet and joyful melodies of nature. Amazingly, this again, was only but a mere week ago. Come today, all had vanished. The once sunny and cheerful garden was now replaced by a dark and gloomy scene; consisting of a bleak and heavy blanket of thick white snow, accompanied by icy frost and the howling winds of winter.

Unfortunately, due to the stormy weather, Kate and her family were advised to shelter in from the piling snow. Determined to find joy even in the most mundane of circumstances, Kate found enjoyment in gazing outside of her frosty window; all in the hopes of catching a rare glimpse of a fallen snowflake. A snowflake, she thought, was so incredibly beautiful and rare, that only a person patient and willing enough to wait for it, could eventually, see it, one day.

"Kate, come away from that window," cried Shakire, her grandmother.

"I need you and Jennifer to help me in the kitchen."

Taking one final glance, Kate hoped for the best. But alas, her hopes were premature; for the winter snow was still progressively falling and there was still no sign of a single snowflake, in near sight.

"We better hurry Kate, I think that she might have a nice surprise for us," said Jennifer, with a twinkle in her eye.

Jennifer was Kate's sister--her twin sister to be precise. Both sisters were identical twins, with the same facial structures, blue eyes, fair complexions, petite body structures and tall in height. However, the only exception between them were their hair colorings, in which Jennifer's hair was naturally blonde, while Kate's was brown. Other than this singular difference, both girls were identical; even down to the very same freckle located right underneath their chins.

However, it wasn't very difficult to distinguish the twin sisters apart; for once they spoke, it became abundantly clear, as to which sister was whom. Jennifer, the lively, romantic and passionate twin, often spoke carefree to whatever and whichever came directly to her mind; whereas, Kate, the practical, shy and reserved twin, analyzed her thoughts and calculated her words more carefully before sharing them publicly with others. While Kate preferred to spend her Saturday nights at home reading a Jane Austen book, along with a warm cup of Earl of Grey tea; Jennifer, in contrast, was more interested on attending parties and finding her modern-day Prince Charming. Due to their opposing natures, Shakire often referred to them as the sun and the moon; in which Jennifer, along with her bright yellow hair, was the sun and Kate, with her shiny and dark hair, the moon. Ironically, this reference was entirely appropriate for them too, since their own given middle names meant exactly that in the Turkish language. Just like the sun, Jennifer was named Jennifer Guneş; and just like the moon, Kate was named Kate Aylin.

At seventeen years old, the twin sisters came to visit Shakire's home for their winter holidays. Located on the northwestern coast of

Türkiye, bordering the Marmara and Aegean Seas, Shakire lived in a small but modest city called Balikesir. Their mother, a native of the land, had married their father, an American soldier, who was previously stationed there in their small town. As a result, the twin sisters were born and raised in New York City. While they primarily resided in New York for their schooling, their winter and summer breaks were spent almost entirely and exclusively in Türkiye with Shakire.

Following their grandmother's directions, the twin sisters walked into their kitchen and saw Shakire already seated at the table. To their surprise, right next to their grandmother, were three separate small cups of coffee. Without their prior knowledge, the warm beverage had already been carefully brewed and poured right into the golden ceramic expresso cups, along with their matching saucers.

"I thought that you needed help?" asked Kate, surprised by the sight before her eyes.

"Actually, I still do," admitted Shakire, with a huge and bright smile, as she took her first sip of coffee. "Although I might have already taken the liberty to prepare us some nice Turkish coffee; now, I'm in need of your help to drink them."

"Wonderful!" exclaimed Jennifer, happily. "Does this mean, what I think it means?"

"Yes, it does," replied Shakire. "Once we finish drinking our coffee, we'll do a little round of fortune telling with the coffee grounds. A nice unexpected treat to a cold and dreary winter's afternoon, don't you think?"

Excitingly, both sisters were happily in agreement. Drinking Turkish coffee was one of their most favorite pastimes at Shakire's home. Coffee time was also their bonding time together. In addition to fortune telling, Shakire also used this opportunity to share tall tales and exotic stories about their history and culture with them; and in return, the sisters also confided about their own secret dreams and life pursuits to their grandmother. Even though their coffee readings were entirely for fun, it was also often claimed by several other family members and nearby neighbors, that Shakire's predictions did actually come true, from time to time. Although Shakire tried her best to teach and share this natural gift to her granddaughters, the art of coffee reading, or tasseography, was something that just came naturally to one's self and wasn't a trait that could really be learned, nor taught. Therefore, rather than attempting to decipher the meaning for themselves, the twin sisters simply quietly sat back and enjoyed themselves, as they listened to Shakire's reading, instead.

"There, I'm done!" shouted Jennifer, as she quickly gulped her last sip of coffee, and then, hastily flipped the empty cup upside down and back onto her saucer. Upon closing the cup, Jennifer promptly spun the object around her in a circle, and then at long last, she made a wish.

"That was fast," observed Kate; who, in contrast, preferred to savor each and every last bit and morsel of her coffee.

"Alright, my dear Jennifer. Let's have a look at it," Shakire instructed.

Following her grandmother's instructions, Jennifer quickly handed her cup and saucer over to Shakire. Upon receiving it, Shakire proceeded to flip the cup right side up; after which, she slowly began to inspect the dried coffee grounds.

"Hmm," began Shakire. "I see several lines in your cup. My dear, I believe that you shall travel the world."

Happy with her grandmother's prediction, Jennifer privately smiled to herself. Unbeknownst to most, Jennifer had secretly dreamed of traveling the world.

"I also see a large diamond ring, with lots of coins," Shakire continued, "You will marry wealthy and also be a very famous woman, at the same time."

Bringing Jennifer's cup even closer towards her, Shakire slowly pulled down her eyeglasses to carefully examine the remaining coffee grounds directly with her naked eye. After a few extra silent minutes of concentration, Shakire finally spoke and said "But…"

"But? Is something wrong?" asked Jennifer, suddenly concerned with the possibility of something being potentially troubling and an exception to perfection.

"Nothing to worry about, my dear," replied Shakire, as she attempted to console her granddaughter. "But," she continued, "I do see two rings. I'm afraid that you will marry twice, after all."

"Twice?" asked Kate, this time, who was equally surprised by this particular revelation.

"Yes, two marriages," Shakire confirmed. "Although you'll marry your first husband at a young age, your second marriage will occur much later on. Unlike your first, your second marriage will be a happier, prosperous and longer union, with wealth and children. He will also be a far better and more ideal match for you, too."

"I suppose that as long as my second husband is far wealthier than the first, then I'm perfectly fine and content with that," laughed Jennifer, not at all bothered by the prospect of marrying twice.

"Either way, I shall record this information into my diary, and in twenty years' time, we'll know as to whether or not you were right," added Jennifer, boldly.

"Jennifer, must you write and record about everything inside of your diary? Our coffee times are meant to be for fun only!" exclaimed Kate.

"Kate, if I'm to become a famous celebrity one day, then I might as well start recording this information now, in time for my future biography. But enough about me, it's time to look at Kate's now," said Jennifer, as she was now determined to shift the focus away from herself and onto her sister.

"Alright my dear Kate, please finish up your cup, and then, let's go ahead and take a look," Shakire instructed.

Under any normal of circumstances, Kate would have much better preferred to have taken her sweet time to savor each and every last sip of her coffee, while eating either a sweet pastry or a chocolate bar on the side. For Kate, preparing, serving and drinking Turkish coffee was an art, in which there was a famous Turkish proverb: a cup of coffee amongst strangers can spark a new lifetime of friendship. And indeed, Kate was a true believer of this very wise, yet true proverb.

Following her grandmother's request, Kate drank the remainder of her coffee. Unlike Jennifer's coffee, which was bubbly and sweet with sugar; Kate drank her coffee plain, strong, dark and bitter. In contrast to Jennifer's sugary coffee style, Kate's coffee's aroma was bold and masculine, and the color of her drink was as dark as charcoal. To top it all off, the rim of her cup was covered by a thick layer of foam; similar to the same sea foam found throughout the Mediterranean Sea.

After taking her final sip, Kate turned her cup upside down onto the saucer to allow her coffee grounds to fall and settle along its surface. Since the shapes and symbols formed by the coffee grounds were meant serve as a helpful guide to her grandmother's fortune telling, Kate took extra care to give a good and thorough spin around. After a few brief moments to allow the coffee grounds to dry, Kate slowly handed her coffee cup and saucer over to her grandmother.

"Thank you, my dear," said Shakire, as she graciously took the cup and saucer from Kate's hands.

While Shakire focused on the coffee cup, Kate sat nervously awaiting her grandmother's predictions. Although Shakire had previously read her coffee grounds a hundred times over; most of the times they were rushed, light-hearted and purely for fun, without much thought or effort. However, today, Shakire appeared to be in a more serious mood. Unlike before, she seemed to be in full concentration and so, Kate wondered if this time, her predictions today were meant to come true.

Lifting the cup up from its saucer, Shakire stared deep into the pits of her coffee grounds. Carefully, she examined each image and symbol with extra care, as she traced each image with her index finger. For a long while, Shakire remained silent, in full concentration. As the clock ticked away, Kate began to wonder and worry as to what was taking her grandmother so long to reveal her predictions.

"Grandmother, are you not finding anything in my cup?" asked Kate, finally, breaking their silence.

"No, I definitely do see something; but Kate, you have a very interesting cup," revealed Shakire, at long last.

"I do see books, a large university, podium, and an audience…you will be a teacher, one day, Kate," Shakire predicted.

"Well, that's to be expected," huffed Jennifer, sarcastically. "We all know as to just how much Kate loves her books and school. But what about marriage?"

Apparently, Jennifer was far more eager to inquire about Kate's future, than Kate was to ask about herself.

"I do see marriage, too," replied Shakire. "But Kate's marriage will come about under very peculiar circumstances; but I dare say, in the end, hers will be a tremendously happy and romantic marriage, indeed."

"Peculiar, in which way?" asked Kate, most curiously.

"Yes, peculiar, in which way?" echoed Jennifer.

"I cannot say for certain," answered Shakire. "But Kate, circumstances beyond your control will bring you to him. Fate, it seems, will cross your paths together, in the most unexpected way. Furthermore, you'll know that it's him, when he first kisses you…in the snow."

"The snow?" exclaimed both Kate and Jennifer, excited by that revelation.

"Yes, the snow," Shakire confirmed. "And Kate, I do see a little snowflake in your cup, too."

"A snowflake?" asked Kate, stunned by this new prediction. How amazing that only but a few minutes ago, Kate sat ever-so patiently staring away at her window, and waiting and hoping to see a snowflake. How strange that her one wish would somehow magically appear inside of her cup?

"Yes," replied Shakire. "There's a snowflake and a very beautiful one at that, I dare say. The edges are rough, but the design is almost as beautiful as a winter rose. And right next to the snowflake, is a lovely white pearl."

"Oh, that's Kate's favorite gem, the pearl," interrupted Jennifer.

"Yes, I know. And next to the snowflake and pearl, is the man," added Shakire.

"Kate is going to marry a snowman," Jennifer playfully teased.

"No, that isn't it," replied Shakire. "Kate, one day, this man is going to fall madly in love you. But first, you have to overcome some obstacles. Like all important tasks, you'll have to climb your mountain, before you acquire your treasure. But in the end, it will be all worth it; for he's your soul mate."

"How romantic!" cried Jennifer. "A kiss in the snow, snowflakes, roses, pearls and all! It must be true love, Kate!"

Kate blushed. Only time would tell.

About the Author

Kristina Stangl is an American author. She was born and raised in San Francisco, California, USA. She holds a Master's degree in Public Administration, MPA; a Bachelor of Arts in International Relations, with a minor in Middle East and Islamic Studies from San Francisco State University; along with Teaching English as a Foreign Language (TEFL) credentials from the University of Toronto, Ontario Institute for Studies in Education. Before writing her first novel, Kristina previously worked in both the public and private sectors, having served in the United States federal government for nine years. In addition to writing, Kristina enjoys traveling across the globe and visiting famous and historical sites, which she documents on her social media accounts. To date, she has traveled to over thirteen countries, three continents, and speaks three languages. When Kristina is not traveling or writing, she's at home experimenting with baking new desserts, pies and other sweet treats.